FALLING for my *Boss*

J.S. COOPER & HELEN COOPER

This book is a work of fiction. Names, characters, places, and incidents either are the product of the author's imagination or are used fictitiously. Any resemblance to actual persons, living or dead, events, or locales is entirely coincidental.

Copyright © 2015 by J.S. Cooper and Helen Cooper

Cover design by Louisa Maggio at LM Creations.

All rights reserved. Except as permitted under the U.S. Copyright Act of 1976, no part of this book may be reproduced, scanned, distributed, or transmitted in any form or by any means, or stored in a database or retrieval system, without the prior written permission of the author.

Also by J. S. Cooper

One-Night Stand

Falling for My Best Friend's Brother

Illusion

Finding My Prince Charming

The Ex Games

The Private Club

Rhett

The Last Boyfriend

Everlasting Sin

Crazy Beautiful Love

About Falling for My Boss

Falling For My Boss is Book One in a two-book series.

Scott Taylor was sex on legs and it took everything that Elizabeth Jeffries had to resist him.

When Elizabeth was hired for a job with her party-gram company, she had no idea that her new boss, Scott Taylor, was going to have such an effect on her. He was a handsome flirt and he liked to push the boundaries of their office relationship. Only Elizabeth, with the guidance of her best friend, decided to push right back. She wanted Scott to know that he wasn't the only one who could play games.

Thus began the ultimate game of cat and mouse. They both began to tease and lure each other into their webs, but then something explosive happened. The games went too far, and Elizabeth was pushed to the limit. Scott didn't know what to think when he found out Elizabeth's big secret and the reason why she took the job. The truth caused everything to blow up and split apart. However, neither one of them were to know that Elizabeth would take another job that would bring her back into his world.

Acknowledgments

First of all thanks to all of the readers that have fallen in love with Liv, Alice, Xander, Aiden, Scott and the gang. I really love these characters and feel so happy that I've been able to continue their stories.

I would like to say thank you to my beta readers Tanya Kay Skaggs, Katrina Jaekley, Stacy Hahn, Kathy Shreve, Chanteal Justice, Charlotte Spence, Cathy Reale, Cilicia White, Elizabeth Rodriguez, Carrie Franks-Fink, Barbara Goodwin, and Kanae Eddings. Thank you for all your help and feedback.

I hope everyone enjoys Elizabeth and Scott's story.

FALLING

for my

Boss

Prologue

One month after both of my acting jobs were finished

"Do you want to know what I'm going to do to you?" His voice was soft as he whispered into my ear. My legs shook and my skin tingled at the feel of his warm breath. He didn't wait for me to answer before he continued talking slowly in a seductive voice. "I'm going to tie you up so you can't move, then I'm going to spray whipped cream on your breasts and then I'm going to—"

"Scott!" I cut him off, my face going red as his sister Liv and her best friend Alice looked at me with confused and interested expressions from across the room, where they were looking at a photo album from their high school days.

"Yes, Elizabeth?" He stepped back and smiled at me innocently.

"Stop it!" I hissed at him when I saw Liv and Alice looking away.

"Stop what?" he said with a smirk and ran his finger across my lips gently.

"You can't do that." My eyes flashed at him as I looked at the two girls again. What was he playing at? Was he going to expose me and the fact that we'd already met? Heat spread across my face and warmed my belly as I stood there in front of him. Oh God, he wasn't going to tell them about our shared past, was he?

"I think you'll find I can do what I want," he said casually and then leaned back down to whisper in my ear again. "And I think after I've sprayed the whipped cream on your breasts and down your stomach, you'll be begging me to do what I'm thinking about doing next."

"What's that?" I swallowed hard, not believing I was allowing myself to question him. Like I even cared about what he was going to say. Like I wanted his lips on me. Again. I shook my head slightly, to remind myself that I certainly did not want his lips on me again. No, sir. No thank you. I didn't need to feel the incredibly hard and sensuous Scott Taylor sliding—

"Are you listening to me, Elizabeth?" He blew in my ear and I jumped back suddenly. "Or should I say, Eliza" —he paused and grinned widely— "Doolittle?"

"What do you want me to say, Scott?" I said, my tone rising as I was unable to stop myself from giving him the reaction I knew he wanted.

"I want you to say that when I fuck you the next time, you won't be playing any games."

"The next time?" My jaw dropped, both at the crudeness of his words and the fact that he thought we were going to get together again.

"Yeah." He smiled and his blue eyes gazed into mine with an amused expression. "Only this time, you'll be the one getting the shock of your life."

Part I

The first time I worked for a Taylor brother.

There are some jobs that you should never accept. No matter how badly you need the money. No matter how attractive your boss may be. There are some jobs you should never take; not if you believe in self-preservation. And not if you have a suspicion that you wouldn't mind sleeping with your boss.

I had to learn this lesson the hard way. Not once, but two times.

J.S. COOPER ✣ HELEN COOPER

Chapter One

"Sex on legs," I mumbled to myself as I stared at the photo, my heart beating fast. The man, Scott Taylor, looked like he was about six foot two, with dark hair and dark, navy blue eyes. There was a five-o'clock shadow on his jawline, and he was glaring into the camera, his lips twisted at the corners in a slight scowl. To say he was sexy was an understatement. This man, this Scott Taylor, was the picture of a perfect man. He looked absolutely gorgeous, and I knew that the photo was affecting my decision of whether or not to take this particular job.

"Lacey," I groaned into the phone. "They want me to dress up like a secretary and then go into his office and give him a lap dance. I just don't know if I can do that." I blushed as I stared at his photo and I knew I was lying. I'd have no problem giving McHottie a lap dance if he were my boyfriend—but he wasn't my boyfriend. I didn't even know him. He didn't even know I existed. And he had no idea that his friends at work were trying to pull a sexy prank on him.

"No way, are you a stripper now?" my best friend, Lacey, asked in a shocked voice. "I thought you only did singing birthday-grams and stuff like that at your job?"

"We do," I sighed. "But my boss sometimes gets special requests and they pay more."

"How much more?"

"Like two hundred dollars," I said, and I groaned again as I fell back on my bed and held Scott Taylor's photo up in the air. "Is two hundred dollars worth losing my dignity over?" I asked Lacey, wishing that she were here in person to give me advice and shake me out of even considering taking on this job. The sad part was that the extra two hundred dollars wasn't the draw; meeting Scott Taylor was.

"There aren't many things I wouldn't do for two hundred dollars," Lacey said, and I laughed. "And trust me, you will never lose your dignity."

"When are you coming to visit me?" I asked her softly, trying not to sound like I was whining. Though I really was. It was miserable not having my best friend close to me.

"Soon," she said in a cheery voice. "Just as soon as I finish my first book."

"You can write here," I said. "And you can stay with me. Rent free."

"Eliza, I love you, but you can barely pay the rent. Imagine if we both got kicked out. Where would we go?"

"I miss you. I wish you would just move here already," I moaned into the phone. Lacey and I had been friends since we were four years old. We became *best* friends at seven, and we sailed through high school and college together, joined at the hip. It was only after college ended that things went awry. I moved away to the city to pursue my lifelong dream of being an actress, and Lacey moved back home to write a book. Or rather I should say, *the book*. The book was going to be a blockbuster. It was going to be so fabulous that every literary agent and publisher would be dying to get their hands on it. Then Lacey would become rich and famous and take care of us until we found husbands. The other plan was for me to star in a blockbuster movie alongside Bradley Cooper and become rich and famous and take care of her. So far, neither of our plans was working. Her book had ten pages and my acting career was non-existent, aside from the roles I played for Candy Canes Birthday Grams. Candy Canes was actually run by a man named Bob Johnson, and he was about as sketchy as you would expect a fifty-five-year-old man with a big beard and a closet full of wife-beaters to be. I'd taken the job because I'd been desperate to make some money, but some of the assignments I'd been given recently seemed shadier and shadier. However, this one was pushing the limit the most. What would it mean to give a lap dance to a stranger? Granted, it was a joke, but would it make me some sort of cheap hussy?

"What are you going to do, Eliza?" Lacey asked me eagerly, and I knew that she loved my dilemma.

"You got the photo I sent you, right? Bob gave it to me to show me the client wasn't some sketchy guy."

"Yes, he's hot. Super hot." Lacey laughed. "You should go for it. I mean, how lucky are you to get paid two hundred dollars to meet him?"

"I'm doing more than meeting him. I'm pretending to be his new secretary, and then I have to give him a lap dance in his office. Then his coworkers will burst into the room and say, 'Surprise!'" I explained to Lacey. "I just don't know if I'm going down some sort of slippery slope if I agree to this job."

"Do it!" She giggled. "What's the worst thing that can happen?"

"You're a bad influence, Lacey." I sat up and shook my head at the phone. We both knew what was the worst thing that could happen. It had already happened to me. But then, that had been the past and this was now. And this was a very different situation. Maybe this was what I needed to get me back into the dating game and feeling more relaxed.

"That's why you love me," she said, and I could picture her light brown eyes crinkling at the corners as she giggled.

"If I take the job, will you come visit? I can use the two hundred to pay for your ticket," I said, ignoring the stirring in my stomach that said that I should put the $200 in the bank.

"That sounds like a deal to me," she agreed. "I can't wait."

"Neither can I," I said softly as I looked at Scott's photo, but *I* wasn't talking about her visit.

✦ ✦ ✦

"So what you going to do, Liz?" Bob's eyebrows furrowed as he gazed at me with eager eyes. He was trying so hard to act as if he didn't care if I said yes or no, but I knew that all he could think about was the money that he was potentially going to pocket. I figured he was getting 50% of whatever was being offered, which was dreadfully unfair, but what could I say or do? Not much, really.

"I'm not sure," I said casually, though I was pretty sure I was going to take the job. I was hoping that by faking nonchalance, Bob would panic and offer me more money. At least that's what the self-help book that I'd been reading had said to do when you wanted your boss to give you a raise: make them think that they were going to lose you (this only worked if you were a valued employee, which I hoped I was).

"You're going to make two hundred dollars." Bob's squinty eyes were almost popping out of his face. I stifled a giggle as I saw the panic cross his face.

"Yeah, but two hundred isn't much. Not worth losing my dignity over." I was lying about the first part.

Two hundred dollars was a lot to me, but I wasn't going to let Bob keep $200 as well, not when I was the one pretending to be a stripper and having to shake my lady bits. I wasn't going to be acting like a stripper for $200, not even if the guy looked like Scott Taylor.

"I thought you said you needed to make every extra penny that you could?" Bob looked at me suspiciously. I knew by the way his eyes narrowed that he was wondering if I was lying.

"I do, but I'm not so desperate that I'm willing to let all my standards go."

"Three hundred, then," he said with an annoyed expression.

"You've got a deal," I said quickly, forgetting my qualms in a heartbeat. Three hundred would help to buy Lacey a plane ticket to come and visit me and would pay off all my monthly bills. I'd almost feel like I was rich, not having to worry about if my electricity was going to get cut off before payday. I knew I always had the option of getting a proper job, a 9-5 that would pay the bills slightly better, but I knew that a 9-5 would never give me the option to go to acting auditions, and without the auditions, I'd never make it as an actress.

"What about two fifty?" Bob said, and I shook my head at him, wondering if he'd lost brain cells in the bill cans stacked in his office.

"You already offered three hundred and I accepted," I said adamantly. "And I want the cash before the job or I'm not doing it."

"You can trust me, Elizabeth," he said and frowned. "No need to be acting all hifalutin on me now. You know you'll get your money."

"I want a stack of twenties in my hand." I pursed my lips and put my hands on my hips. "Without them, I don't take this job."

"I can get someone else to do it, you know," he said in a huff, but we both knew he was lying. Bob only had three other employees: one was a middle-aged man who thought he was the second coming of Hulk Hogan, another was a lady in her early seventies, and I was pretty sure she was the Hulk's mom, and then there was Jessica. Jessica was eighteen and a bookworm. She used all the money she made to buy books. She wore big owl-like glasses, baggy jeans and had never been on a date. I knew that there was no way in hell that she'd take the job. And Bob was too cheap to hire anyone else.

"Oh, okay then." I smiled sweetly. "If that's what you want to do." I turned around and walked towards the door. "I'm going to go get the clown costume for the birthday party this afternoon. See you later."

"Wait!" Bob's voice sounded panicked. "You can have the job with Scott Taylor. I offered it to you first. It wouldn't be fair to you if I let Jessica have it."

"Yeah, thanks, Bob." I rolled my eyes before turning around to look at him. "Have my money ready tomorrow, and we'll have a deal."

✦ ✦ ✦

"Do you have my money, Bob?" I stood in the doorway to his office and raised an eyebrow. He was busy stuffing his face with a Big Mac, and I was half worried he'd spent my money on the dollar menu at McDonalds as he had so many bags on his table.

"The bank could only give me two hundred," he said as lettuce flew from his mouth. I looked away as my stomach rumbled and I tried not to laugh.

"Oh, did they run out of money?" I said and then looked back at him, my right hand on my hip.

"Yeah," he nodded, his beady eyes looking at me carefully. "So I can only give you two hundred."

"Well, I guess you'd better call Jessica and see if she can do the job." I turned around. "Oh, and join a bank that is able to provide its customers with more than two hundred dollars at a time."

"Wait, wait!" Bob jumped up, and I turned around again. "I spoke to the manager, and he was able to get them to give me another hundred."

"Uh huh," I said, wondering what sort of fool he thought I was. "Where's the money?" I held my hand out and waited. Bob looked annoyed, and I could tell that he was trying to think of something else to say to keep some of the money.

"Here you go." Bob handed me a stack of bills, and I frowned when I looked down and saw a bunch of ones. What a jackass! "Now, you also have to sign a nondisclosure form."

"What?" I narrowed my eyes. "Why?"

"You're not allowed to tell your new boss that his friends hired you as a gag."

"I'm not going to tell him," I said, exasperated. "Well, not until the fake lap dance and the reveal when his friends burst into the room at the end of the day."

"That's kind of changed," Bob said as he handed me a piece of paper and a pen. "Sign here."

I looked at the contract and saw that the client's name was "H. Smith." I frowned and then signed the paper quickly and then looked up at him. "What's changed?"

"Well, you're not going to reveal yourself right away." He grabbed the paper back from me.

"Hmm, okay?" I frowned, not understanding.

"The guys who are hiring us think it will be even funnier if you work there for a week and give him the lap dance at an office meeting."

"What?" My voice expressed my horror. "Are you joking?"

"No." He grinned. "I told them that won't be a problem."

"I'm not working there for a week for three hundred dollars." My voice rose. "You can't make me do this, Bob."

"You just signed the contract." He shrugged and walked back to his desk. "And you took the money already."

"For a one-day job, not a one-week job," I protested. "This isn't right, Bob, and it seems unfair to Scott Taylor as well. A week is a long time to fool someone, and the whole 'lap dance at an office meeting' seems sleazy."

"We don't create the rules, we just follow them."

"These aren't *rules*, Bob. This is ridiculous."

"I thought you said you were a good actress?" He paused and gave me a questioning look, and I could feel my stomach curdling. "A good actress can take on any job."

"I am a good actress," I retorted back to him. I hated when he pressured me into these roles. In fact, I hated Bob. I knew I needed to get a new job, but I'd just been too lazy to find one.

"Then take this job and shut up," he said as he sat back down on his chair and started eating some French fries.

"You're an asshole," I said and was about to leave the office when he said the words that changed everything.

"You'll get paid three hundred a day for a week," he said and I froze. Was he being serious? Three hundred a day was a lot of dough.

"So I start on a Monday and end on a Friday?"

"You start next Monday," he said as he took a large sip of Diet Coke (oh, the irony). "You'll be in training as the secretary and flirting all week. The office party is on a Saturday. You'll go to the party, give him a dirty lap dance and then his friends will come in and tell him 'surprise,' and your job will be done."

"Uhm, what's a dirty lap dance?" I frowned, my heart racing. Everything seemed simple enough except for the dirty lap dance. What exactly were these guys hoping was going to happen, and why?

"A lap dance in a short skirt and a bikini top."

"Are you joking?" I glared at him. "Bikini top?"

"Pretend you're acting in *Dreamgirls* with Elizabeth Berkeley." He paused from eating, and I watched as his eyes glazed over. "Maybe you should even watch that movie for some tips." He swallowed hard as he daydreamed. "Watch how she swings her hips when she's in the casino. And then when she bends back and she rubs her titties in his face and he's motorboating. Hmm."

"Bob!" I shouted, feeling sick to my stomach. "Are you out of your mind?"

"Oops, I got carried away." He looked at me guiltily. "Sorry."

"Uh huh," I muttered, feeling like I needed a shower.

"Just watch some movies, learn the moves, and show up on Monday and do your job," he said and then opened a file. "We have some birthday parties coming up this weekend. Do you think you'll be able to dress up as an elephant on Saturday?"

"An elephant?" I shook my head. "No."

"I guess I can ask Jessica." He made a face. "Okay, you can go now."

"When am I going to get the rest of the money?" I asked him, pausing before I left the office.

"They'll pay you at work," he said with a face, and I knew he was telling the truth then because of how upset he looked. I knew he was upset because that meant he wasn't getting his grubby hands on more of my money.

"So I just show up to the office on Monday and say I'm reporting for work as Scott Taylor's new assistant?"

"Yup. I'll email you the address."

"And he won't find this suspicious?"

"Nope." He shook his head. "Oh yeah, wear a sexy suit to work on Monday."

"What?"

"Remember, your job is to seduce him so he lets you give him the lap dance on Saturday at the party."

"I don't really understand how this is going to be funny." I sighed. I knew that Bob didn't care what I thought, but I seriously didn't know what sort of joke this was meant to be. This wasn't something that I'd done before working for Bob and his Candy Grams business. It seemed to me that Bob was taking on more and more clients that weren't just simple birthday surprises. I was starting to worry that I was letting Bob lead me down a slippery slope. What was he going to ask me to do next? Slip out of a cake naked and offer me five hundred dollars?

"It's not our business." Bob shrugged. "We just take the money."

"Is that really the way we want to lead our lives?" I asked him softly. "Doing whatever we have to to make money? Do we want to sell our souls for a few bucks?"

"I don't know about you," Bob said as he munched on some more fries, "but I think I'd be happy to get paid to flirt with a hot guy if I was you. You seem like you don't get much action by yourself."

"Goodbye, Bob," I said angrily and turned to leave his office for good before I went off on him but then turned back to him with an afterthought. "By the way, I want a copy of that contract I just signed."

"Yeah, yeah. I'll email it to you." Bob rolled his eyes and I left the office wondering what I was getting myself into. I quickly grabbed my phone to call Lacey to help me calm down.

✦ ✦ ✦

"Thank you for calling Wet 'n' Wild, where the women are wet and the men are wild," Lacey answered the phone in a sing-songy voice, and I groaned.

"Not now, Lacey."

"Uh oh, what's wrong?"

"My boss is a jerk, and I think he's going to try and sell me into prostitution or something."

"Sell you into prostitution?"

"Or the slave trade or whatever," I said grumpily. "I think I'm making a mistake."

"You mean the stripper job?"

"It's not a stripper job," I whined. "I'm going to be his assistant for a week, and then I'm going to give him a quick lap dance at an office meeting and then his friends are going to burst in and say 'surprise' or something like that."

"What's so wrong with that?" Lacey asked innocently. "It's just a job."

"I know it's just a job, but he looks hot and, well, what if something happens?"

"What do you mean?" Lacey said in a light tone. "What could happen?"

"What if he gets hard during the lap dance or something? Or, you know."

"No, what?" she asked excitedly.

"What if I like it?" I groaned, thinking of the photo. "He did look very attractive."

"Girl, you sound like a desperado." Lacey laughed. "Go on a date with one of those guys from online and concentrate on them instead of this guy that you don't even know."

"I don't want to meet any of those guys," I sighed as I got into my car. "They just don't seem like my type."

"You never know until you meet them," Lacey said matter-of-factly. "And what about that one guy, Mike? He looked like he was a hottie. You need to get out there, Elizabeth. You can spend the rest of your life thinking about you know who."

"Yeah, true, he looked hot in his military uniform, though his face was partially hidden." I didn't acknowledge her dig at my ex, Shane. She was right in that he wasn't worth thinking about. Not anymore.

"He serves our country, Eliza, he deserves a date with you."

"I guess." I laughed. "Anything to thank him for his service."

"See, if you have a hot soldier boyfriend, you're not going to care about some guy you're fake-working for."

"I don't think Mike is going to become my boyfriend in less than a week," I said with a sigh, but I was smiling as I drove back home. "You're a goof."

"You won't be saying that if he asks you to marry him this weekend."

"Lacey, give me a fat chance, I haven't even met him yet."

"Meet him this weekend—that way when you start your job on Monday, you'll have someone to daydream and think about and won't get caught up in your fake boss."

"Yeah, I guess that's true." I nodded. "Okay, I'll message him back tonight and see if he wants to meet up Friday night or something."

"Good idea, and before you know it, you'll have a proper acting job and can tell Bob and his sleazy ways to kiss off."

"I can't wait for that day," I said wistfully as I thought about the job I'd just accepted. I knew it wasn't exactly a night-worker job, but I still didn't feel very good about the fact that I'd taken a job where I knew I had to give the guy a lap dance. I didn't even care that he looked like he was going to be hot. Well, not completely.

Chapter Two

"Wear the lace panties and don't forget to shave." Lacey giggled into the phone.

"Lace panties?" I said. "Don't you mean a silk thong?" I questioned her and then spoke again before she could answer. "And just in case you got the wrong impression, I'm not wearing a silk thong, either. They are so uncomfortable, and I don't even know this guy, Lacey. This is our first date. He's not even going to have the opportunity to see my panties, silk or otherwise."

"Stop being a grandma." Lacey didn't sound impressed. "You need to get laid. It's been way too long for you."

"Not by some guy I've never met before. He could be a serial killer or a rapist. Online dating isn't so safe anymore, Lacey."

"Was it ever safe, Eliza?" Lacey questioned me, and I ignored her.

"And I'm not shaving, either," I said indignantly, though technically that was a lie because I'd already shaved.

"Well, make sure you get a wax, at least," Lacey said. "And go full-Brazilian, please, no landing strip—you're not in the jungle, and you don't want a hippie."

"You're talking about my vagina?" My jaw dropped. "I thought you were talking about my legs. Are you out of your bloody mind, Lacey? I'm not shaving off all my pubes for some guy off OkCupid that may or may not look like his profile."

"Okay, Tarzan's wife, let him explore in the jungle and get lost. Maybe his snake will find your lost gorilla?"

"You're disgusting, Lacey." I laughed. "Mike is not getting into my pants."

"Be prepared for every possibility, Eliza, you know what your mom always says."

"I am a lady," I said indignantly, in a cockney English accent, trying very much to sound like my idol, Audrey Hepburn, in *My Fair Lady*.

"I know, I know, you're a good girl." Lacey laughed. "You're not a freak like me."

"A freak?" I groaned and giggled at the same time. "Have you been listening to Ludacris?"

"Don't try to change the subject, Elizabeth. You need to just let loose and have some fun."

"I will when you come and visit or better yet, when you move here."

"You just want me to go crazy so you can go crazy, too."

"Well, it's always easier with a wing woman."

"I know," Lacey said, and she paused. "I do want to move closer—you know that, right?" She sighed. "I just don't want to come until I can carry my own weight and pay my own bills. I don't want you to think that I'm taking advantage of you."

"I know," I said softly and sat down on my couch as I spoke into the phone. "You know that I don't have much, so you wouldn't be taking advantage. I just want you here. It's hard not having my best friend here to tell me when I'm being an idiot and helping me choose what outfits to wear on my nonexistent dates."

"You have a date tonight, so not nonexistent," Lacey said, her voice wistful. "Unlike me. I never have a date."

"Well, come here, and we can go on dates together. We can even go speed dating."

"Speed dating?" Lacey said, and I could almost picture the surprised look on her face. "You would go speed dating with me?"

"Yeah, if you moved here."

"I'm going to hold you to that, even if everything goes well with Mike."

"Yeah, we'll see." I sighed as I pulled out my makeup bag. "I just don't know what's going to happen with Mike. I just have a feeling that something is a little off."

"Don't be a pessimist," Lacey said, her voice bossy. "You're going to have fun tonight. You're going to have the time of your life on a hot date and you're going to have all the guys wishing they were Mike."

"Yeah, we'll see," I groaned. "Okay, I'll call you on the way there. I have to finish getting ready."

"Okay, I'll be waiting," Lacey said, and I hung up on her and looked at myself in the mirror and then sighed as I walked to my closet. I was going to dress sexy, even though I didn't really want to. However, Lacey was right, I needed to get out of my own skin. I needed to have a real relationship. And if Mike was as down to earth as he seemed in his profile, then maybe he could be the one. Anything was better than me showing up to my new gig on Monday, lusting over a guy I'd only seen in a photo.

✦ ✦ ✦

"Why do I listen to you?" I moaned into the phone as I walked towards the bar/restaurant in my short black skirt.

"Because if he's hot, you'll be thankful that you're looking sexy."

"There's a fine line between sexy and a skank," I huffed as I stopped outside the bar. "Okay, I have to go now," I said as I looked at my watch. "He should be waiting for me inside."

"Call me as soon as the date is done and don't do anything I wouldn't do," Lacey said excitedly. "Oh, and try and text me a photo of him as well. I want to see if he looks as good in person as he does online."

"I'm not taking a photo of some guy I'm meeting for the first time from online. Are you crazy?"

"Do it casually," Lacey said impatiently. "You don't have to make it obvious."

"Yeah, 'cause there are a million reasons why my camera would be in front of his face at a bar," I said. "Anyways, I have to go. I'll call you afterwards."

"Did you forward me the contract you said you signed?" Lacey asked quickly, and I stopped outside the main door.

"Yes, I did. It'll be in your email. I'll call you later, okay?" I hung up before she could answer and took a deep breath. I wasn't sure exactly what I was going to say when I met Mike. We'd only exchanged two messages before he'd asked to meet, and I'd let Lacey talk me into accepting. It wasn't like I had much else going on in my life right now. I felt like a tramp as I walked into the bar with my short black skirt, black heels and white halter top that accentuated my boobs without completely exposing them. I walked towards the bar and ignored the looks from a group of middle-aged bikers that were staring at my legs. I was grateful for the looks of appreciation, but slightly disappointed as well. I was disappointed because there was a cute—from the back—man sitting at the bar and he hadn't even glanced in my direction. I held in an exasperated sigh and looked around for my date, Mike. My heart immediately sank as I saw a balding man in a big leather jacket grinning at me with a glass of something in his hands. *Oh God, please don't let that be Mike*, I thought to myself as I stifled a groan. I wasn't Miss America, but this man looked twenty years older than his photos, and he looked like a redneck—and not the cute NASCAR, 'I'm a cowboy' kind, either. This was no Jimmie Johnson. This was definitely Bubba, and my heart sank as he walked towards me.

"Why, is that you, Elizabeth?" My heart dropped at his words and the large gap at the front of his mouth.

"Howdy," I said and groaned under my breath. I had no idea why I was talking country.

"Why, aren't you a large spray of sunshine on a sunny day," he said as he reached over to give me a hug. *Spray of sunshine?* I thought to myself. What in hell was he talking about?

"Uh, thanks," I said as I gave him a quick hug. I watched his eyes dropping to my chest before he whistled.

"Thank you, God, you've gone and blessed me today," he said as he licked his lips loudly. "Girl, you're fine," he said, and I was almost positive I could see saliva on his lips. Gross.

"Mike?" I said weakly. Please, God, if you love me, let this be a mistake.

"Yessiree, that is me." He grinned and rubbed his hands together. "I didn't know nothing 'bout this online dating thing, but I'm God-dang sure I won the lottery."

"Oh, ha ha." I attempted a laugh as my heart sank. "Where are you from?"

"Originally from N'awlins, by way of Alabama," he said, and I had no idea what that meant.

"Oh, okay, are you new to town?" I asked, wondering how long I'd have to stay on this date. I was even more annoyed that I'd used my home waxing kit down under, now. I was starting to feel an itch and I knew I couldn't scratch it. I was sure going to kill Lacey.

"Came up here for my ex wife." He nodded. "I'm a country boy, if you didn't know, but I came for love and didn't leave."

"Your profile says you were never married," I said accusingly, finally able to comment on something other than his looks. I wanted to call him out on his lies, but I didn't want to be rude.

"Oh, we wasn't married in a church." He took a sip of his drink. "We just says we were married for tax purposes."

"Uh okay." I looked away from him and I could see that the man at the end of the bar was now staring at us in interest. I looked away from him quickly, even though he looked slightly familiar. I didn't know why, though. I didn't know any hunky dark-haired guys that looked like him.

"But that's over now. Tammy's gone to 'sippi with George, a guy I used to work with."

"Sippi?" I asked him, confused, not sure if I was being punked.

"Mississippi," he said and grinned. "Guess you're a natural blonde after all." And then, because he was gross, he looked down to the front of my skirt. I was about to tell him where to get off when I felt someone behind us.

"You okay, miss?" The voice was deep and husky, and I instantly knew it was the man who had been sitting at the end of the bar.

"She's fine." Mike sounded annoyed and possessive, and I took a step away from him.

"Ooof," said the man behind me as I bumped into him. His arms instinctively went around my waist as I stumbled back against his hard, warm chest.

"Sorry," I said and looked back to see his face properly. His azure blue eyes stared into mine as he looked at me with an amused expression. My heart jumped as I realized that I was standing in front of Scott Taylor. Only, I couldn't tell him that I knew his name. If I did, he'd want to know how, and I wasn't allowed to tell him about the prank that his friends were about to pull on him.

"No worries," he said, his hands sliding off my waist slowly. "You okay?"

"I'm fine." I nodded, and then we both looked back at Mike, who looked anything but fine.

"Looky here, boy, can't you see I'm on a date?" he said, and it was then that I realized he was chewing tobacco. That was why I'd seen the saliva on his lips earlier, not because he was drooling because I was so hot.

"You okay?" Scott Taylor ignored Mike and addressed me again. I shook my head slightly, not wanting to say anything out loud for fear of Mike doing something stupid.

"She's fine." Mike took a step forward. "Get away from my lady."

"I'm not your lady," I said finally and looked at him in disgust. "We barely messaged twice online, and you were lying!" My voice rose. "You don't look thirty and you don't look like your photos."

"My photos say they were of me when I was in the marines." He shrugged. "That weren't no lie."

"But it also wasn't yesterday, was it, sir?" Scott spoke up and stepped in front of me. "How's about you leave the young lady alone. You're obviously not what she was expecting."

"Hmmphm, damn Yankees," Mike said under his breath and looked back at me. "You sure you don't wanna learn how a cowboy moves his hips tonight?" He licked his lips again. "I might be older, but I make up for it with my tongue."

"What?" My jaw dropped as I stared at him.

"I can't last all night in the sack unless I take my Viagra, but my tongue can go for hours." He flicked his tongue around. "If you know what I mean."

I turned away from him then, shuddering in disgust. Lacey was going to be in fits of laughter when I told her about my night. Only I was going to kill her before that. Never again was I going to take her dating advice.

"Come, let me get you a drink," Scott said, and he guided me to his seat. I could feel Mike's eyes on my back, but I didn't care. I was sure that anyone else watching us was wondering what was going on, but it was none if their business.

"Before I buy you a drink, I must ask you a question," Scott said with a small smile. I wanted to pinch myself. Was I really here with the man I was hired to prank next week? Was fate playing a dreadful joke on me?

"What's that?" I asked him as I sat down, wishing I could check a mirror to make sure my makeup still looked good. My heart thudded as I stared at him. He was even better looking in person than he'd been in the photo.

"You weren't on a sugar daddy website or anything like that, right?" he asked me with a cheeky grin.

"No," I said with a laugh and shook my head.

"Or 'get an old man now and take all his money in a few years dot com'?"

"Ha ha, no."

"Good." He smiled and held out his hand. "Then let me introduce myself properly. My name is Scott."

"Elizabeth," I said with a smile. "Though my best friend calls me Eliza, like Eliza Doolittle from *My Fair Lady*."

"Because you're a good girl?" he asked with a wink, and I flushed as he laughed. "You didn't think a man like me would know the movie, did you?"

"No, yes, no." I laughed. "But no, I didn't think most people would really know that line where she says she's a good girl. It's so obscure and forgettable."

"But I'm sure you're not forgettable."

"Are we talking about me or are we talking about the movie?" I asked softly, my face reddening.

"Both," he said with a smile. "It's not often I get to flirt with a hot girl at a NASCAR bar."

"NASCAR?" I looked around and groaned out loud. "This is a country bar, huh? No wonder Mike invited me to meet him here."

"Yeah," Scott nodded. "I was supposed to meet my brother Chett here for some drinks, but he got stuck at work."

"Oh, that sucks," I said.

"Not really." He laughed. "I'd much rather save a hot girl from a creep than have to listen to my brother talking about Gordon and The King."

"I'm guessing Gordon is Jeff Gordon, but who is The King?"

"Richard Petty, of course." He laughed. "Do you follow racing?"

"Not really." I shook my head. "My best friend used to have a crush on Jimmie Johnson, so I know him, but not much else."

"Good." He laughed. "I don't follow it, either. My brother Aiden and my sister Liv always joke that my brother Chett must have been adopted, because he's the only one that cares anything about the sport."

"Sounds like you have a big family," I said, wanting to pinch myself for my good luck. How was I so lucky that I'd gone on a crappy internet date and met this hunk? The same hunk I'd been salivating to Lacey on the phone over a couple of nights before. What would he think if he knew that I already kinda knew who he was? Would he be freaked out? I so wanted to tell him that I'd been hired to surprise him, but knew I couldn't spoil it.

"Yeah, pretty big. We're all pretty close." He nodded. "But enough about them, tell me more about you, Eliza."

"What do you want to know?" I asked him softly as I flicked my hair back.

"What do you want to drink?" he said as he leaned towards me. "And what is a good looking girl like you doing meeting weirdos at bars?"

"I'll have a Malibu Sprite, and are you calling yourself a weirdo?" I lowered my voice to sound as seductive as I could and he laughed as he stared at my lips.

"I can be whatever you want me to be." He leaned closer and I could feel his breath on my lips. "I can be a race-car driver, a football player—shit, I can even be a cowboy if you want."

"You'll say 'yeehaw' for me?" I teased him as I batted my eyelashes up at him.

"I'll say 'yeehaw' and 'giddy up' and show you how to catch a hog with a piece of string if that's what you want," he said as he reached over and wiped something off of the side of my face. I wasn't sure if there was really something there or if he just wanted a reason to touch me.

"Quite forward, aren't you?" My skin was tingling from the feel of his warm fingers and I wondered just how far he was willing to take this flirtation. Not only that, I wondered just how far I was willing to take it. Especially seeing as I knew that come Monday morning, I'd be in his office as his new assistant.

"When I see someone I like."

"Like, or want?" I said breathlessly, not knowing where my bravado was coming from but feeling quite proud of myself.

"Would it be rude of me to say both?" His mouth shifted to my ear and he blew in it gently. "Would it be rude of me to tell you that I'd love to take you right here and now, on the bar?"

I gasped and pulled away from him, my eyes flashing as I gazed at his laughing face.

"I'm taking that as a yes," he said as he sat back down and took a swig of his beer. "It doesn't hurt to ask, does it?"

"I'm starting to think you're as bad as Mike."

"You mean Bubba?" he asked me with a grin.

"You're horrible, but yes." I laughed.

"I might be as bad, but at least I come in a nicer package, right?" He winked at me and then looked down at the front of his pants. "If you know what I mean."

I wasn't sure how to answer him. All I could do was stop myself from looking down at his package as well.

"Have I offended you?" Scott said quickly, making an apologetic face. "I'm sorry if I did. My sister says I can be a bit out of control sometimes."

"Only sometimes?" I asked him with a small smile, looking into his eyes, but still feeling an urge to look south.

"Well, she thinks it's only sometimes." He laughed. "But she's one to talk, since she and her best friend, Alice, are super inappropriate."

"Sounds like me and my best friend, Lacey," I said with a smile, knowing that Lacey was most probably staring at her phone right now, wondering what was happening on my date.

"Oh, you like to be inappropriate, too?"

"You could say that," I said with a small smile, wondering what I was playing at. I felt like I was playing a game that I shouldn't be playing. It just didn't seem fair that I would meet and be attracted to Scott just days before I was about to become his fake assistant for a week and give him an office lap dance. I squirmed in my seat as I thought about giving him the lap dance. That wasn't going to be hard at all. In fact, it was going to be a fun experience. The only problem was I didn't know if I'd be able to keep my hands off of Scott until then. Not that that was a problem, of course. At least it wasn't to me.

Chapter Three

"Another drink?" Scott asked me with a lazy smile as we sat at the bar talking about movies.

"No, I should get going," I said, though I didn't really want to go. I was really into Scott, both physically and mentally, and I really just wanted to spend the next few hours talking to him, but I didn't want to look too eager. It was weird that I was enjoying his company this much. I was usually too scared to let my guard down with a new guy, but there was something about Scott that just made me want to be with him.

"Aw, do you have to work tomorrow?" he asked as he gazed into my eyes, his right hand on my knee.

"No," I said softly and I could feel my skin tingling as he ran his hand up my thigh. "No work tomorrow."

"Oh, that's good." His hand felt warm as it moved farther up my thigh and I was about to slap it away when he lowered it back to my kneecap. "What do you do, by the way?"

"I'm an actress," I said softly, hoping he didn't ask too many questions. I didn't want to talk about either of our jobs. I didn't want it to get messy. Which was a bit of a joke because it was going to get messy when I showed up at his office the next week. Hopefully, he would think it was a cool coincidence.

"Oh?" He looked surprised.

"I know this isn't Hollywood, but there are a lot of jobs here," I explained, almost defensively. No one really understood why I hadn't moved to Los Angeles when I'd decided to pursue my acting career. Not my mom. Not Shane. No one but Lacey had been supportive of my move.

"Well, that's good," he said as he put his arm around my shoulders. "Want to leave this joint and check out my apartment?"

"To see your art etchings in your art studio?" I asked him lightly, teasing him to see how he would react, and I was surprised when he burst out laughing.

"Something like that. Too forward again?" His expression looked worried as he stared at me, and I did something next that shocked both of us. I leaned forward and lightly pressed my lips against his and kissed him. I wasn't sure what had come over me and was about to pull back when he deepened the kiss and pulled me towards him. I felt his hand at the back of my head, running through my hair and tugging it slightly roughly. He groaned against my lips before slipping his tongue inside of my mouth. His tongue tasted like a pecan-flavored pear, and I kissed him back eagerly, throwing all caution to the wind. A voice in the back of my head was cheering me on, as my own body couldn't even believe that I was making out with a strange guy in a bar. I moaned slightly as Scott stood up and pulled away from me. I looked up at him with hazy eyes and pouted.

"Don't pout, beautiful," he said as he grabbed my hands and pulled me off of my stool and into his arms.

"I'm not beautiful," I mumbled, but the top of my ears were burning in joy as I stood there.

"And modest, too." He grinned and pulled me towards him even more, so that my body was pressed firmly against his. "You sure wore a sexy outfit to a blind date," he said as his hands slid to my ass.

"What are you doing?" I gasped as he squeezed my butt cheeks.

"Feeling up on your butt," he said huskily, his eyes burning into mine.

"Don't you think that's inappropriate?" I said and then gasped even louder as he pushed my butt so that I was pressed up against his hardness.

"*This* is inappropriate," he said as he turned me around so that my back was against the bar. He grabbed my legs and lifted me up slightly. "Put your arms around my neck," he whispered into my ear.

"No," I said, but my arms didn't listen as they curled around his neck and played with his hair.

"Good girl." He pushed himself into me. "Wrap your legs around my waist."

"Yeah, right." I laughed and pushed him away. I could feel his heart beating from his chest and he stepped back with a wry smile on his face.

"Aww. I was hoping this would be my lucky day." He winked at me and then leaned down and gave me another long and lingering kiss. "But maybe it already has been," he said as his fingers played with my hair.

"You're a flirt." I shook my head and smiled up at him lazily. I felt like I was in some sort of romance movie and I loved it.

"So are you." He stroked my hair. "So what do you say? Want to go back to my place?"

"Hmmm, but I barely know you."

"My name is Scott Taylor. I'm single. I think you're cute," he said with an impish smile. "I'd like to have my wicked way with you."

"I can't believe you just said that!"

"What can I say?" He winked. "I'm honest as well."

"I don't know what to say to that." I bit my lower lip. "I'm not really a one-night-stand kinda girl."

"Neither am I." His eyes glowed. "But then again, I'm not a girl, either."

"That's good." I laughed, my heart racing as we just stood there staring at each other, waiting to see what the other person was going to do next.

"You don't have to come home with me," he said finally. "I mean, you can also come, and we don't have to have sex."

"We'll just watch movies?"

"Yeah, or play board games. I have Twister." He grinned.

"Naked Twister, right?"

"I could be persuaded," he said, his voice husky as his fingers played with mine. "So what do you say, Eliza Doolittle? Are you going to come home with me for a night of debauchery?"

"I shouldn't." I shook my head, my heart pumping rapidly.

"Do you always do things you should do?"

"I don't know you."

"You said that already." He leaned down and kissed my lips. "And you know me a little bit."

"I'm not that kind of girl," I said again, being repetitive in my words and thoughts.

"I'm that kind of guy." He grinned and then ran his fingers down the side of my body. "Spend the night with me, Eliza Doolittle. Get to know me. Let me get to know you. You might find that we like each other."

"There's something I should tell you," I said and took a big breath. "Something you should know—"

"Unless it's you telling me you're married or in a relationship, then there is nothing I need to know." He shook his head and kissed my lips hard before pulling back. "The only other thing I need to know is if you like it slow or fast."

"Oh," I said, feeling my face going red as I gazed back at him in shock. I didn't know what else to say. In fact, I remained silent as he dropped some cash on the bar and led me out of the restaurant and to his car. I knew I was being incredibly stupid by going with a strange man, but in that moment I didn't care. In that moment all I wanted to know was just how fast was fast and just how slow was slow.

Chapter Four

I felt like a giddy schoolgirl as I entered Scott's house. I looked inside eagerly and was surprised to see that it was clean and tidy. In fact, it was in immaculate condition, and I wondered at how a guy could be cleaner than me. It was a bit embarrassing to admit that his house was better put together than mine, but then he looked like he had a lot more money than I did as well.

"Welcome to my humble abode," he said with a grin as he closed the door behind me. "Would you like another drink?"

"No, thanks," I said and stared at the photos on the brick mantelpiece. "Are these your brothers and sisters?" The photos were surrounded by little souvenirs from what I assumed were his travels. I looked down and saw some dark spots in the fireplace and realized that it was a working fireplace.

"Yes." He nodded. "That's the entire clan: Chett, Aiden, Gabby, and Liv." He pointed them out in the photo and smiled lovingly as he looked at his family members.

"Who's the other girl?" I asked, slightly jealous as I wondered if that was Scott's girlfriend. "There are three girls in the photo."

"That's my sister's best friend, Alice. She's like my sister, and may very well be one day." He grinned then.

"Oh?"

"She and my brother have a thing for each other." He walked over to his big white couch and sat down. "If they ever figure it out, that is." He rolled his eyes and waved me over to him.

"They don't know?"

"My brother is waiting for her to grow up or something before he makes a move." Scott rolled his eyes. "He doesn't know how to just go for what he wants."

"Unlike you, right?" I grinned as I walked over to the couch and sat next to him. It was soft and comfortable, and I leaned back into the soft cushions and gazed in front of me. He had a big reclaimed wood coffee table with some magazines on it. I could see *GQ* and some car magazine. There was an old beer bottle on top of the *GQ* and some peanut shells on the table. I grinned to myself as I realized he wasn't a total clean freak.

"I go for what I want." He nodded and undid his tie. "What's the point in wasting time?"

"So what do you want?" I asked softly as I watched his nimble fingers pulling his tie off. I wanted to reach out and touch it to see how soft it was, but I didn't.

"A hot blonde in my bed tonight," he said and started to unbutton his shirt. I could see some small dark chest hairs on top of his golden skin and I swallowed hard. He really was sexy as hell.

"Does she have to be a natural blonde?" I reached over and undid the rest of the buttons on his shirt. I wanted to text Lacey and tell her how forward I was being. I knew she wouldn't believe that it was actually me here on this couch. She wouldn't believe that I, Elizabeth Jeffries, was letting go and just going for what I wanted. She'd be proud of me, but she wouldn't believe it.

"Depends," he said, and he grabbed my fingers and ran them down his hard abs.

"On what?" I asked breathlessly.

"Depends on if you're one or not."

"Oh," I said and scratched my fingernails across his nipples.

"Oh, you're Catwoman, huh?" He licked his lips, and I felt his fingers rubbing against my stomach as he pulled my halter-top up.

"Not really," I said and leaned down and took his nipple in my mouth and sucked it. I heard and felt his intake of breath and grinned. "Ooh," I said as I felt his hands pulling me onto his lap and sliding up my ass. "What are you doing?"

"You're not the only one who can be a tease." He sucked on my earlobe as his hands pulled my skirt up. I could feel his hands molding my butt cheeks as his fingers slipped inside of my panties. I groaned inwardly as I remembered I was wearing boy shorts as opposed to a sexy thong.

"No, I'm not," I said as I reached down and rubbed the front of his pants. He felt thick and hard beneath my fingers and I swallowed hard.

"Like what you feel?" he said with a grin, and it was then that I realized that he was as cocky as he was hot.

"Perhaps."

"Only perhaps?" He raised an eyebrow and jumped up. I watched in amusement as he pulled his pants and boxers down in one fell swoop. I stared at his naked cock and swallowed hard again as it flopped around in front of me. It was magnificent and I was slightly overwhelmed as I stared at it.

"What do you think now?" he said and grabbed my hand and pulled it towards his manhood. I placed my fingers around it gently and ran my fingers up and down his shaft.

"It's not bad," I said silkily, and he laughed as he sat back down next to me.

"Not bad, huh?"

"That's what I said." My fingers clasped his cock tighter and he groaned as he leaned back against the couch.

"Lie down," he said in a commanding voice and pushed me back. "Lie on your back."

"Why?" I asked huskily as I lay back.

"You'll see," he said as he stared down at me, completely naked. "Put your hands up," he said, and I did as he told me. He pulled my halter top off and I watched as he bent down and pushed my naked breasts together, his fingers gently rubbing against my nipples. I groaned as I felt him slide his cock between my breasts and the tip of his manhood brushed up against my chin and lips as he moved back and forth. "You're so fucking sexy," he said, and I watched as he grabbed the length of his cock and rubbed the tip of it against my mouth. "Suck me," he said and I opened my mouth slightly. I sat up a little as he pushed his cock into my mouth. It tasted salty and felt hard as I sucked on it, and he groaned loudly as I took him in farther and farther. I couldn't believe that I was sucking on his hardness already and enjoying it. Everything was going so quickly, but I didn't care. It felt good and it felt right. Things seemed to go by in a blur and I felt high on power when he pulled his cock out of my mouth and exploded on my chest, his hot sperm spewing all over my breasts.

"Come with me," he said softly as he grabbed my hands and pulled me on some stairs with him. I followed him into his bedroom, and he picked me up and threw me down on his bed. I looked up at him and he was grinning down at me as he reached down and pulled my skirt and panties off in one quick movement. "Let me see," he groaned as he leaned down and got onto the bed.

"See what?" I whispered as my naked body shivered slightly.

"Let me see if you taste as good as you look." He winked and then I felt him spreading my legs before burying his face in my pussy.

"Oh, Scott!" I cried out, not knowing what to say, aside from his name, as I squirmed on the bed. "Scott!" I screamed as his tongue entered me, sliding in and out of me so delicately and powerfully that it felt better than any dildo I'd ever used. I felt myself getting close to orgasm, when he suddenly pulled out of me. "Don't stop," I moaned, and he grinned down at me. I watched him reach out to his night table and heard the ripping of a wrapper. I knew he was putting a condom on. I knew he was about to fuck me. I was about to have sex with a man I barely knew and I didn't care.

My body felt feverish. I felt high on lust and pleasure and all I wanted was to feel him inside of me.

"Is this what you want?" He grunted as he pulled my legs up over his shoulders and positioned himself at my entrance. "Is this what you want, Elizabeth?" The tip of his cock rubbed against my clit, and I squirmed against him. "Tell me what you want," he growled down at me.

"You—I want you!" I screamed, unable to take it anymore. And that was when he thrust into me, so hard and steady. His cock slid into me smoothly and seemed to fill me up completely. He moved in and out of me skillfully, and I felt so much pleasure that I didn't know which way was up and which way was down.

"Come for me, Elizabeth," he growled as he continued to move in and out of me, his fingers rubbing my clit aggressively as my breasts jiggled. His eyes were intense as he looked down at me and he growled in satisfaction as I climaxed hard and fast on his bed. It was only then that he pushed me back up on the bed and collapsed down on top of me and fucked me harder and faster. I knew then that he'd been waiting on me to come before he would allow himself to release again. I wrapped my legs around his waist while he slammed into me and I felt like a queen as I felt his body jerking when he came inside of me. I watched as he rolled over, pulled the condom off and lay back next to me, panting.

"Now *that's* what I call a good fucking," he said as he looked at me with a smile.

"You can say that again," I said with a small laugh and then I squealed as he rolled me on top of him and I felt his cock growing hard against my wetness once again.

✦ ✦ ✦

"So, about last night." Scott's voice was soft as I opened my eyes the next morning.

"Hmm, what about it?" I asked and stretched in his sheets, feeling warm and satiated with him next to my body.

"It was pretty hot, don't you think?"

"Yeah." I nodded, suddenly feeling shy as I thought about all the different things we'd done.

"And I'm not judging you." He leaned down and kissed me as his hand crept to my breast.

"Judging me?" I kissed him back and ran my hands down to his butt.

"For sleeping with me on the first night." He laughed against my lips and yelped as I slapped his butt.

"Hey, you're lucky I'm not judging you," I moaned as I felt his fingers slip down from my breast to the valley between my legs. The valley that was already wet.

"I love morning sex." Scott grunted as his fingers reached my wetness and he rubbed my clit gently.

"Who said you're getting morning sex?" I asked as my back arched on the bed.

"The woman I picked up last night kinda hinted that to me." He laughed as he kissed down my stomach.

"She did?" I whimpered as his lips found my wetness and his tongue eagerly licked me up. I closed my eyes and my fingers gripped the sheets as he sucked gently on my clit. I shifted on the bed and spread my legs and cried out in wild abandon. I felt free and happy. This was my first time letting loose and just giving myself to a guy right away. It felt exhilarating and freeing and I couldn't wait to call Lacey and tell her just how hot my night had been. I felt Scott's tongue slide inside of me and I screamed out as he entered me with as much passion as his cock had had the previous evening. It was only when he removed his tongue and sat up that I realized that his phone was ringing off the hook. I groaned as I watched him roll over and grab it. He looked at the screen and frowned before looking back down at me.

"Sorry, it's work." He looked away from me and I felt my stomach curdling at the sudden change in mood.

"Oh no, everything okay?"

"Not really." He sighed and jumped out of the bed. "I think they need me to work today because I, uh, I'm leaving the country for a month next week and they want to make sure that everything in the office is left intact."

"You're going away?" I asked, my heart sinking as I stared up at him. I pulled the sheets up over my naked body and tried to control my breathing.

"Yeah." He nodded. "Work trip, like I said. Uhm, but I'll call you when I get back, and we can go to dinner."

"I see." I bit on my lower lip and tried not to cry. What was going on?

"Just a second." He looked at me guiltily. "I have to go to the bathroom." He dropped his phone on the mattress next to me and hurried out of the room. I watched him leave the room, and I quickly grabbed his phone. It was locked, but I could see that he had ten missed calls from someone called Helen Smith. My heart thudded as I wondered who she was and why was she calling him. Even more importantly, why had his mood changed so quickly and why was he lying to me? The previous night had been so good, so sensual and exciting. I'd thought we'd had a lot in common, even though we'd just met. I'd thought that this could go somewhere. I'd even been planning to reveal to him that his friends had hired me for an office prank. I'd wanted to tell him everything, so that we could really get to know each other. I'd thought that perhaps this could really go somewhere.

"Sorry about that," he said as he walked back into the bedroom, his cock swinging loosely in front of him. I couldn't stop myself from looking at it. He had a perfect cock. It was almost majestic in the daylight. Long, thick—but not too thick—and the tip was shaped like a perfect, peachy mushroom. I licked my lips involuntarily as I remembered how good it had tasted. I felt a feeling of shame spreading through me as I realized that I wanted him in my mouth again. I wanted to feel that same heady power that I'd felt the night before when he'd begged me to not stop sucking on him. I could still hear his growls as he spurted hot come all over my breasts. I could still feel the softness of the warm towel he'd used to gently wipe his come off of my nipples. And then when he'd entered me, it had felt like we were one. His cock had moved inside of me as if it knew every inch of me intimately and it seemed to know all the secret spots to turn me on. I sighed as I looked up at him. It couldn't have just been sex, could it? It had to have meant more than that.

"Is everything okay?" I asked again, praying he would burst out laughing and fall down on the bed next to me.

"Uh, not really," he said and his expression looked pained. "I would love to have breakfast with you." He sat down on the bed and looked into my eyes with a sad expression. "But I have to go in to work."

"I see," I said, my stomach dropping. So he was continuing with his lies.

"I had a great time last night," he said, and he reached over and touched my cheek. "It was special."

"Yeah, sure," I said and looked away from him.

"If it wasn't for this job," he sighed, "I'd like to see where this could go—really, I would."

"Uh huh."

"Give me your number, and I'll call you when I'm back in town, okay?"

"Yeah, sure you will."

"Don't be like that, Eliza," he said with a frown as he tried to kiss me. I avoided his lips and sat up.

"It's Elizabeth." I jumped up out of the bed and quickly looked for my clothes. "Well, it was nice meeting you, Scott," I said quickly as I pulled my skirt on. "Have a good work trip."

"Elizabeth, please," he said and I felt his hands on my waist. "Don't be mad at me. You don't understand."

"I understand enough, jerk," I whispered under my breath and grabbed my handbag. "I'm leaving. I'm glad you had a good night."

"It's not like that," he pleaded, but I turned around and glared at him.

"Whatever." I gave him one last haughty glance and hurried down the stairs so that I could exit his house quickly. "And don't follow me out!" I shouted as I heard him behind me. I saw him standing there, looking upset, but I didn't care. He was the one who had used me for a one-night stand. He was the one who had lied. I hurried out of the door and slammed it shut, before running down the road and stopping at the corner so that I could hail an Uber from my phone app. I waited for the car to pull up before texting Lacey and telling her I was going to kill her. I wasn't sure how I stopped myself from crying, but I didn't shed a tear until I stepped through my own front door. And then I went straight to the bathroom and turned on the faucet so that I could soak away my tears and passion.

Chapter Five

"You can shout at me," Lacey said when I called her on Sunday morning. "It was my fault you went on the date."

"I'm not going to shout at you." I moaned. "It's not your fault I'm a slut."

"You're not a slut," she said, and I knew she was worried about my state of mind. Ever since Shane, Lacey had been worried that I was going to break down. She didn't understand that that wouldn't happen again because I wouldn't let myself get into that position again.

"Lacey, I went on a blind date, ditched the date, met another guy and went home with him and had sex with him. That's the definition of slut."

"No, it's not. If you'd gone home with him and let him fuck you in the ass on a first date, then I would call you a slut."

"Lacey," my voice was soft, "you're calling me a slut, then."

"Oh. My. God. You let him do anal?" she screamed, and I couldn't stop myself from laughing.

"No, but the shock in your voice letting you think that for a few seconds was priceless."

"You're horrible." She giggled, but I could tell that she was no longer worried that I was in a deep, dark depression. "Are you going to be okay?"

"Well, I mean tomorrow's going to be awkward," I said sarcastically. "Can you imagine what his face is going to look like when I walk into his office as his new assistant?"

"You're not going to tell him that his ex-girlfriend hired you?" Lacey asked questioningly.

"Nope," I said vehemently. "Helen Smith, or H. Smith as she calls herself on the contract, is paying a lot of money for me to embarrass him at the office meeting on Saturday. I don't want to disappoint her."

"But she lied!" Lacey exclaimed. "Bob told you this was set up by Scott's friends as a joke, but we know Helen Smith is actually Scott's ex-girlfriend, and I doubt she is doing this as a joke."

"Well, that's his tough luck," I said bitterly. "I'm sure she has her reasons. And good detective work, by the way."

"It wasn't hard." She laughed. "Scott's Facebook page isn't private, and he has old photos with her."

"But it was detective work that led you to confirming that Helen Smith was the H. Smith. Not many people would have looked up criminal and civil records to match a signature."

"You know me, I'm thorough." Lacey laughed modestly. "But we really don't know what happened between them. Maybe you should tell him what's going on. Maybe he had a reason to lie."

"He lied because he wanted to hit it and quit it, and maybe he's trying to get back with Helen," I said with a groan. "Well, I'll show him."

"What are you going to do?" Lacey asked, her voice breathless. "And are you sure you want to? Didn't you say he was the best sex you've ever had?"

"He was all right," I lied, not wanting to remember just how good he'd been. "And I'm going to do what Helen asked. I'm going to go in and be his assistant. I'm going to pretend I don't care that he lied, and then on Saturday, I'm going to give him the lap dance of his life and embarrass the shit out of him."

"Oh, Eliza, you sound like you have a plan."

"Well, you know what they say about plans…" I grinned into the phone. "Don't reveal them if you want them to come true."

"Eliza, what are you going to do?"

"Can't say just yet." I laughed. "But look, I have to go and choose my outfit for tomorrow. I want to make sure I'm looking my best when Scott Taylor lays eyes on me for the second time."

✦ ✦ ✦

My heart was racing as I waited outside of the office. I could see Scott sitting at his desk in a dark navy-blue suit. He was on the phone and scribbling something down on a piece of paper. My heart thudded as I stood there waiting for him to call me inside. I couldn't wait to see his eyes as he recognized me. I couldn't wait to see the shock and to hear the excuses. I couldn't wait to bend over to pick up a pen so he could stare at my long legs and pert ass. I was going to drive him crazy and I was going to love it. He would pay for using me for a quickie. I knocked on the door and waited.

"Come in," he called out without looking up. I walked in to the room slowly and stopped a couple of yards away from his desk, waiting for him to look up and see me. He held a hand up as he continued talking on the phone, and I could feel my stomach rumbling as

I waited for the moment our eyes would meet. "Sorry about that," he said finally as he hung up the phone. "I'm Scott Taylor," he said and stood up, his hand outstretched. I watched as his blue eyes widened in shock and his jaw fell open. He looked at me for a few seconds and then smiled widely. "Well, well, well, look who we have here," he said with a huge grin that had my stomach doing somersaults. I had no idea why he looked so happy to see me. Didn't he realize he'd now been busted?

"Scott?" My jaw dropped as I faked surprise. "I thought you went away for business?" I said and took a step towards him. "What are you doing here?"

"Elizabeth Jeffries, you're my new assistant?" His eyes narrowed as he stared at me, and I watched as he walked out from behind his desk and over to me. "Now, now, today is my lucky day." He reached out, grabbed my hands and pulled me towards him.

"What are you doing?" I asked in shock as I felt his warm, hard body against mine.

"Continuing where we left off," he said with an impish grin as his hands fell to my ass. "I've always dreamed of an office quickie." I stood there in shock, not believing my ears. How could Scott Taylor flirt and act like everything was okay? How could he put his hands on me and think I'd just pick up where we'd left off the other morning—the morning he'd lied to me? Nothing was going as I thought it would. He wasn't speechless. He wasn't embarrassed. He wasn't stumbling with more lies. If anything, he seemed excited—as if all of his dreams had come true. As if I were some sex toy at his disposal. I could feel my face reddening as I grew angry. This was not what I'd expected at all. However, I started to smile as a new idea came to me. A new plan hatched in my mind as his hands squeezed my butt as if he owned it, and I looked up at him and smiled.

"Well, wouldn't you know, that's something I've always dreamed of as well," I said with a sweet smile. I grinned when he gasped in shock as I reached down, grabbed his cock and squeezed hard. I was going to show Scott Taylor who he was dealing with. By the time I left his office at the end of the week, I was going to have him on his knees.

Chapter Six

Scott and I stood there next to his desk, our bodies shifting against each other comfortably. I could almost believe that he was a good guy and deserving of my body next to his. I could almost believe that it would be okay to let him bend me over his desk and take me from behind. I could almost believe that because I wanted it to happen as well. My heart was beating for him, my breath was raspy imagining him doing things to me and my skin was warm in remembered pleasure.

"I knew you were a freak," Scott said as his hands slid up my shirt and went to cup my breasts. I stood there for a second before I took a deep breath and pushed him away.

"I guess you don't always know what you think you know," I said with a smirk and looked up at him with narrowed eyes.

"What?" He frowned down at me in confusion. I knew that he wasn't sure what had caused the about-face.

"Uhm, what?" I repeated and stood there with my arms crossed.

"Are we not cool, then?" he said, his eyes now narrowed as he looked back at me.

"No, we're not," I said and smoothed my skirt down. "We lost our coolness the moment you lied to me and told me you were going out of town."

"I can explain." He sighed and gave me a boyish smile.

"Yeah, not interested," I said and looked at the clock on his desk. "I'm here for work and that's it."

"I see." He frowned and moved back to his desk. "Are you mad at me?"

"What's there to be mad about?" I said and sat down in one of the chairs. Was he an idiot? Of course I was mad at him. Who wouldn't be mad at him? I'd caught him in a bold-faced lie. I couldn't believe that he was even talking to me with a straight face. What was he thinking? Sometimes I really wondered if men were completely clueless at times. Absolutely, completely, and thoroughly clueless.

"I can explain why I said that ..." His voice trailed off and he sighed as he looked at my hard face. "You don't care for me to explain anything, right?"

"Yeah, we should just keep this professional, don't you think?" I said and sat back and crossed my legs. I held in a smile as I noticed his eyes darting to my legs.

"Yeah, sure," he said and looked back into my eyes. "If that's what you want."

"That's what I want." I nodded, my stomach jumping with excitement. I was starting to feel gleeful inside. I was almost positive my plan was going to work. I was going to play hot and cold all week, and then at the office party, I was going to give him the lap dance of his life. And then I was going to make him think that he was going to get lucky. I'd get him naked. Naked and ready to fuck. And then his co workers could come in and he'd be embarrassed. He'd be completely humiliated and then, and only then, would I feel better about the fact that he'd used me for a one-night stand and then lied to me. A part of me felt guilty. A part of me felt that his punishment didn't fit the crime he'd committed. I mean, I was acting like a woman scorned, almost as bad as Glenn Close in *Fatal Attraction*. Well, maybe not as bad as Glenn Close. I wasn't going to do anything horrible, and it wasn't as if he didn't deserve a little humiliation for lying to me. And it wasn't as if this had been my idea. I'd just been hired for a job, and I was just doing what I'd been hired to do. There was nothing wrong with just doing my job.

✦ ✦ ✦

"I need you to read these papers and sign them." Scott slammed a stack of papers on my desk as he walked out of his office. I looked up at him and tried not to roll my eyes at him. He hadn't seemed to take my rejection very well. I'd been sitting at this desk for the last two hours doing nothing but staring at my nails and wishing I'd worn a different color nail polish. I'd been too scared to take my phone out of my bag to call or text Lacey, and I hadn't known the password to unlock the computer on my desk, so I hadn't been able to go online.

"What's this?" I asked as I looked at the huge stack on my desk.

"Read them and see," he said in a dismissive tone as he turned around.

"Sure, boss," I said in a sarcastic voice.

"The papers will explain your duties," he said as he walked back to my desk. "Are you going to have an attitude with me all day, Elizabeth?"

"I don't think I have an attitude, period," I said and pulled back my chair. I gazed up at him as I stood up and I watched his eyes flittering down the front of my body, his eyes taking extra time to move over my chest area and down my legs. "Looking for something?" I asked bravely, and I watched as his eyes made their way back to mine. His blue irises pierced into mine and I could see the sides of his lips twitching.

"No," he said and walked towards me, stopping right in front of me. He grabbed my hands and pulled me up out of my chair. "Give me your phone," he said, and I frowned at him, my heart racing from being so close to him again. I could feel the warmth of his body radiating next to mine.

"Uhm, what?" I said, my voice sounding feebler that I would have liked.

"I need to give you my number," he said as he held his hand out. "And I need to get yours."

"Why?" I said as I stared at his lips. My mind went back to our night of fun and I wished that, in that moment, we were still there in the throes of passion instead of in this office. It had been such a magical night—until he'd spoiled it.

"Because I might need to call you about work."

"We can't just talk about work at work?"

"You don't want to stay in this job long, do you?" he said with a snide tone, and I wanted to laugh in his face. Little did he know how true his words were. I wondered what he would say if I replied, "No, dickhead, I'm not planning on staying at this crappy job as your assistant for longer than a week."

"It's a pity your acting career didn't work out," he said with a smirk. "But I guess money is more important than a few bit parts at the local theater."

"Excuse me?" I said, my eyes burning into his. "I'm not a 'bit part at the local theater' sort of actor."

"Oh, sorry, you've indulged in pornos, too?"

"What is your problem?" I asked him, extremely annoyed. I was unsure as to why he was being such an asshole. Was this his real personality? If so, I was lucky that our 'relationship' hadn't gone very far.

"I'm just joking, Elizabeth. Don't you have a sense of humor?"

"Obviously not." I grabbed my phone and handed it to him. "Put your number in."

"Why, thank you, ma'am."

Of course, I'm dirty, so the first thought in my mind was, 'Wham bam, thank you, ma'am.' However, I just stood there and watched him putting his number in my phone and then texting himself. I sighed internally, why couldn't he have been trying to get my number because he liked me and wanted to take me on a date? A proper date with flowers and chocolates. I shook my head slightly to stop myself from feeling sorry for the situation I was now in.

"Okay, done," he said and handed me my phone back with a grin. "Now, get to work."

"I'm *trying* to work." I rolled my eyes. "Maybe we can talk about the job you want me to do and not my phone number."

Scott just stared at me then and started laughing, his head tilted back as his gruff, sexy laughter escaped from his throat.

"What's so funny?" I asked him with narrowed eyes.

"You just remind me of my sister, that's all." He grinned. "The younger one, not the older one."

"I don't know either of them, so that means nothing."

"My sister Liv, the one I talked about. You remind me of her, all indignant and annoyed with me. She's always annoyed with me." He laughed.

"I wonder why." I stared at him. "Do you always laugh at her, too?"

"Yes." He grinned boyishly. "That's what a brother has to do to bratty little sisters."

"I'm not your little sister."

"Trust me, I know," he said and licked his lips. I wasn't sure if he'd done that deliberately, but as I watched the tip of his tongue darting across his pink, luscious lips, I shivered. "You should meet her. I think you'd get along."

"That's okay." I shook my head. I had no interest in meeting his sister. I didn't want to get stuck in a world where memories of Scott were all around me. I was going to do this job for a week and then I was going to peace out. I was going to be gone, without a trace as to what had really happened. I'd be the girl who had come into his life and then drifted away into the night. I smiled to myself as I thought about him coming to work the next week and wondering what had happened. He'd most probably try and punish me for what I was planning to do on Saturday—maybe even threaten my job, or try and fire me. Little did he know that he wouldn't have the opportunity. I wouldn't be back after Saturday. "Is there anything you need me to do for the office party on Saturday?" I asked him with a small smile as I changed the subject.

"The office party?" He frowned as he looked at me. "Did I mention an office party?" His eyes narrowed as he looked at me and my heart thudded. Had I said too much? Did he know why I was here? Oh God, I could never be a spy. The FBI, CIA, KGB, MI5 would never want me. I was a royal disaster. A traitor to national security. My face was burning red as I stood there. I couldn't believe that I had slipped up already. "Are you okay, Elizabeth?" Scott's eyes looked concerned. "You look sick."

"Stomach bug." I rubbed my stomach, looked down and took a deep breath. *Get it together, Eliza*, I lectured myself mentally. "And you didn't tell me about the party. I heard some girls talking about it as I got to work this morning."

"Oh, okay." He nodded. "I guess all the secretaries are excited. Everyone loves an office party with free booze and scandalous moments."

"Scandalous moments?" My heart stilled.

"Yeah." He laughed. "Every year, someone gets cursed out or caught kissing. And then everyone in the office is talking about it the following week."

"Oh, wow." I looked up and gave him a small smile. Little did he know that next week the gossip was going to be all about him. I wasn't sure he'd be laughing then. "I'm ready to start working, by the way. Whatever you need me to do, I'm game for."

"That's what I like to hear." He grinned at me and for a moment, I forgot that I hated him and his handsome face. "Does that mean you're game for some morning sex?"

"What?" I screeched, and he just laughed and walked back into his office. I followed behind him, feeling hot and bothered and mad as hell. Not at him for being so inappropriate, but more so at myself for wanting to bend over his desk and let him take me from behind.

✦ ✦ ✦

"How was day one?" Lacey asked me, her tone excited and anxious at the same time, and I didn't know whether to laugh or cry. Lacey was one of those people who always wanted the best for her friends, but she also enjoyed a bit of drama. And when I say a bit, I mean a lot. There's a reason why she's my best friend and a writer. Lacey was the friend who would tell you to do something crazy because she wanted to see what would happen, but then when you were about to do it, she'd beg you to stop because she'd feel worried and guilty that it wasn't going to go well. That's honestly one of the reasons why I love her. Lacey gave me strength by encouraging me to do the things I secretly wanted to do but didn't dare. It was amazing what having her in my life had done for me. She'd shown me how to fly; she hadn't given me the wings, but she'd showed me that I had them.

"It was hard," I said truthfully. "I'm not sure I'm cut out to be the modern day Pussy Galore," I continued quickly, before she could be all encouraging and tell me that it was going to get easier. I didn't want to hear that it was going to get easier. The only thing that could possibly get easier was me—and Scott's ability to get into my pants again. "The character from James Bond, by the way. Not some hooker."

"I knew that." Lacey laughed. "I'm the one that introduced you to James Bond, back in high school, when I liked that guy, Jason Connery, whose dad looked like Sean Connery. Remember I made you watch all those Sean Connery movies because I was going to try and impress Jason with my knowledge of all his dad's movies? And then we realized his dad owned that used car dealership and his name was Shawnie Connery and we laughed because his name was a city."

"Oh yeah," I laughed. "How could I forget Shawnie Connery and the weekend of James Bond and Indiana Jones?" I giggled, thinking back to that weekend and how we'd practiced remembering lines for Lacey to impress Jason with. "Well, then you know exactly what I mean when I say I'm not Pussy Galore," I said and I heard Lacey giggling, most probably because I'd said pussy again. "I'm not sure I'm cut out to play a role like this." I groaned. "He wanted to have sex in his office this morning, and it was hell telling him no. I thought my panties were going to drop off when I saw him."

"Wow, really? They were going to drop off because he's so incredibly sexy? Even panties know the allure of Scott Taylor!" She giggled and I sighed.

"You do not even know, Lacey. He's just so hot and he has this twinkle in his eyes. Argh. When he looks at me and smiles, I feel like my heart is going to explode and it's like we have this connection. And did I tell you how blue his eyes are? They're almost magical. They're intoxicating. I literally feel like I'm floating in the ocean when I stare at him."

"And you don't want to drown, do you?" Lacey said. "He lied to you, Liza," Lacey said, her tone strong. I knew she was being serious now. She only called me Liza when she was being serious. "You don't want a guy that lies; trust me, they aren't worth it."

"I know," I sighed. "It's just so hard."

"It's hard, but not as hard as it will be if you give in to temptation and get your heart broken. Don't make me come down there," she threatened.

"Are you going to come?" I asked her eagerly, hopeful.

"Soon," she said. "I'll be there soon," she said again and then added, "And trust me, you don't want me to come because I'm consoling you because you're crying day and night and knocked up with a baby on the way." I groaned inwardly as Lacey went into her dramatic mode.

"Yeah, you'd better come before I do something stupid and make a fool of myself."

"You wouldn't do that," Lacey said unconvincingly.

"You know I have and I would." I laughed.

"So what's your plan of action, then?" she asked me curiously.

"Exactly what I was paid for," I said and tried not to sigh. "I'm going to lightly flirt and tease, then on

Saturday I'm going to give him a sexy lap dance and get him aroused at his office party and embarrass him."

"But couldn't he get in trouble?" Lacey sounded concerned. "Now we know his ex hired you and not his friends, we know that it's not intended to be a joke. At least not a funny one."

"That's his problem, not mine," I said and pouted, though internally I was feeling a tinge of guilt. Did Scott really deserve to be the subject of gossip the next week, just because we'd had sex and he'd made up an excuse for me to leave? "He lied to me, he most probably is a player that makes girls feel like he likes them so he can have a one-night stand and then he ditches them," I said, trying to convince myself that I was in the right.

"You think so?" Lacey said, trying to play devil's advocate.

"I *know* so," I said adamantly. "Trust me on that. He's a jerk. On the way home from the bar, he was talking about his sister Liv and how she has some crush on some guy called Xander and how he doesn't know how this guy Xander puts up with her."

"And?" Lacey asked, confused.

"There is no 'and.' That in itself is so rude," I said heatedly. "The fact that he is sticking up for another man and not his sister says a lot about him."

"I guess," Lacey said slowly. "What did his sister and this guy Xander do?"

"What do you mean?"

"What's their story? Like, why does he feel sorry for the guy?"

"I have no clue," I said and tried to remember what he'd said. "Something complicated, though. You know how relationships are. I think they met at a wedding or something, but something happened."

"Ooh, I wonder what?" Lacey asked eagerly, and I knew she was dying for some gossip. Lacey was the only person I knew who was as excited by gossip about people she didn't know as she was about people she did know.

"No idea," I said. "And hey, do you think I should go through with this or not? It seems to me like you're having doubts."

"I don't know," Lacey said. "I mean, at first I was, like, yeah, bring his ass down a couple of notches. Who is he to lie to you? Jackass. But now, I'm, like, is this a case of sour grapes on your side? But then I remember that someone else hired you for this job before you'd even met him, so it's not really sour grapes."

"So do it or don't do it?" I said, wanting her to tell me what to do. I just didn't want to listen to myself anymore. I wasn't sure if I was going through with this job for the right reasons or not. I liked Scott Taylor. He seemed fun. I knew he was sexy. However, he was my boss and he was a man I knew I shouldn't fall for.

"Go for it," Lacey said, her answer being the definitive decision to the matter. "I think it will be great. I think you'll show Hottie-McTottie Scott Taylor that he can't just sleep with you, mess you around, and expect everything's going to be okay. And it's only a week. Just remind yourself that this is a job. And on Saturday, make him feel the embarrassment you felt. Let the shame burn through him as he does the walk of shame out of his office party."

"Yeah." I nodded to myself with a smile. "He's going to walk out of that room with the biggest boner, and I'm going to just stand there and smile as he runs out in shame."

"Thata girl," Lacey said and then laughed. "Now I have to go write, but call me later tonight. We have to watch *The Bachelor* together."

"Will do. Bye," I said and hung up. I smiled again to myself as I headed home. Lacey was right. It was only a week. What could go wrong in a week? I'd have some fun with him and then I'd be out of his life. By this time next week, we would have both forgotten about each other.

Chapter Seven

I settled into my couch and turned the TV on and grabbed my phone to call Lacey so we could watch *The Bachelor* together. It was a pretty sad thing to do, but we loved watching trashy TV shows at the same time and talking about them as we watched. When we lived in the same city, we did it together in person, one of us going over to the other's house and bringing ice cream and pizza as we settled in for a night of laughter and fun; but now we had to settle for FaceTime chats and whatever snacks we had in our own fridges.

"Hey, it's me," I said as she accepted my FaceTime request. I loved the fact that we could video chat as we watched the show without having to sit near a computer.

"Hey, you." Lacey grinned into the phone, and I could see a tub of cookies and cream ice cream next to her. I felt very jealous as I stared at the tub. All of a sudden, I wanted ice cream myself, only I wasn't lucky enough to have any in my freezer.

"You're eating ice cream in bed?" I raised an eyebrow at her. "Rough day?"

"Ugh." She nodded and sighed, her long dark curly hair looking messy around her face. "Very long."

"What happened?" I asked as I paused the TV. "Sorry I didn't ask earlier."

"I'm just fed up about everything." She sighed. "My book doesn't seem to be going anywhere, and I don't know what I'm doing with my life anymore. I don't have a husband, I'm not even close to getting married. I have no boyfriend. No money. No nothing. I just feel like a loser."

"You're not a loser, Lacey." I frowned into the phone and lay back, making sure to hold the phone above me so she could see my face.

"You have to say that," she moaned as she started eating her ice cream. "You're my best friend."

"Yes, I'm your best friend, but I don't have to say that," I said. "You just have writer's block, that's all." I tried to look at her face to see if she looked depressed or if she was just feeling sorry for herself. That was the only downside with being on the phone. I never really knew what Lacey was feeling if she was down and we were on the phone. She was a good actress and knew how to put a mask on her face. The only way I knew if she was really okay was if I looked into her eyes.

"Yeah, I guess." She channeled another spoonful of ice cream into her mouth and then smiled into the phone, her brown eyes looking light and mischievous. I felt myself relaxing as I saw her goofy smile. She was okay. I knew it was irrational of me, but sometimes I got worried about Lacey. She was always so chipper, but I knew that she held a lot of insecurities, and when she got low, she got really low. She was my rock, and I tried my hardest to be the same for her. It was weird how close we were as friends; we'd often talked about what we would do if one of us dated a guy that the other one didn't like. We both said our friendship came first, but we'd never been tested. I often worried that a man would break up our terrific friendship, and I despaired that it was me who would be the weak one.

"What's so funny?" I asked her suspiciously as Lacey started laughing into the phone. "What are you thinking about?" I asked her, wondering why she was looking so happy all of a sudden.

"I wonder what Scott is going to say when he finds out you're not really his secretary and rather a sexy actress there to seduce him," Lacey said, and I wondered if she was changing the subject because she didn't want us to focus on her during the call.

"Uhm, first of all, I'm not really an actress, or at least I'm not a working actress, and secondly, I haven't been hired to seduce him. It's not like I'm going to go in there and bend over his desk and say 'take me from behind.'"

"Why not?" Lacey grinned. "It's not like you haven't had sex with him already."

"I can't believe you said that." I shook my head at her. "You're no longer my best friend."

"Why not?" She continued grinning. "Because I know you too well?"

"Bitch." I laughed and groaned. "You do know me too well, and yes, a part of me is asking myself why I don't just have some fun with him this week and to hell with it."

"Well, why can't you have the best of both worlds? I mean, you thought he was good in bed, right? Why don't you have your fun with him this week and then on Saturday give him the lap dance and walk out of his life and make him feel like the biggest fool to hit the planet."

"You mean I should play him?"

"Yup." She nodded as she scooped more ice cream into her mouth. "Play the player."

"That sounds like the name of a movie." I giggled. "Or a really corny book."

"Maybe I should write *that* instead of my current book." Lacey's eyes lit up. "I'd have a guy called Scott, who was tall, blond, and fit with bright blue eyes and he'd meet an innocent sweet girl called Elizabeth, and he'd try to play her, but she would resist and then—"

"You've gotten one thing wrong," I said, cutting her off. I jumped off of the couch and walked to the kitchen to see what junk food I had. Watching her eating her ice cream was making me hungry.

"Oh?" She frowned.

"There's no way *Elizabeth* would resist." I laughed. "Not if he's tall and blond, and sexy, and rich, and fit."

"She's a good girl," Lacey said. "All the girls in romance books are good girls, that's why the men want them so badly."

"Maybe that's what I'm doing wrong?" I said as I opened my fridge. "I'm a bad girl, and I'm getting the bad guys."

"You said Scott was good in bed. So not a completely bad guy," Lacey said, and I rolled my eyes.

"He was hot as hell in bed—he was better than good—but that doesn't mean he's a good guy. Or that I'm a good girl. I acted slutty and I got a jackass."

"Nothing wrong with slutty," Lacey said, and I frowned into the phone.

"Wrong response; this is when you're supposed to tell me that I'm not a slut."

"Oh, yeah, my bad. You're not a slut."

"That sounds very reassuring." I shook my head and laughed. "I'm almost as bad as the girls on *The Bachelor*."

"Hey, not all of them are sluts. Some of them are sweet."

"Which ones?" I asked with a grin.

"Uhm …" Lacey paused, and I could tell she was thinking.

"Hey, I'm getting a call," I said as my phone beeped. "Oh damn, it's Scott," I said as I looked at the screen.

"Ooh, Mr. Bad boy himself. Answer it and hurry back and tell me what he wanted," she said eagerly, and I watched as she jumped off of her bed. "I'm going to get some wine while I wait," she explained as she walked through her parents' corridor.

"Okay, hold on," I said and took a deep breath as my heart raced. "Hello, this is Elizabeth speaking," I said, acting nonchalant.

"Where are you?" Scott's voice was annoyed as I answered the phone.

"Sorry, what?" I asked, confused. What had happened to 'hello' and the other niceties?

"Where are you, Elizabeth?" Scott's voice was a monotone, and I frowned into the phone. What was he talking about? And with such an attitude, as well.

"Watching TV on my couch," I said and sat up. "Why?"

"Isn't there somewhere else you're supposed to be right now?"

"Uhm, in bed?" I asked, confused.

"Didn't you read the work contract?" Scott asked again, his tone suddenly amused.

"What did I miss?" I said curiously and then my jaw dropped as I thought about what could have been a part of the contract. "You're not saying that sleeping with you is part of the job, are you?"

"Would that be so bad?" he asked, his tone teasing. "I thought that would be a perk."

"Not really," I said, my tone dismissive as my heart raced. Was he being serious?

"Well, it's a good thing I'm not asking that of you, then, isn't it?"

"So why are you calling me?"

"You were supposed to come over tonight for some dictation."

"Dick-tation?" I screeched, my heart thudding and then I realized I'd heard him wrong. "Oh, sorry, you mean dictation."

"Yes, Elizabeth. *Dictation*. Which is one of your job duties. And as your contract said, you're required to work some nights as well, at my home office."

"I, uh, must have missed that." I bit my lower lip and looked at the TV. I really didn't want to miss *The Bachelor* as I knew that tonight's episode was supposed to be juicy from the previews and the show was about to start. "Do you want me to come over now?" I offered, but it was clear from my tone that it was a half-hearted offer.

"No, it's fine," he said with a huff, as if he were doing me a favor. "However, I do expect you to come over tomorrow."

"After work?"

"That's what I said, Elizabeth," he said, snapping at me. "Do you have a problem understanding English?"

"That's not exactly what you said," I growled into the phone. "You're an asshole," I said. "Do you have a problem understanding that?"

"That's not an appropriate way to speak to your boss, especially seeing as today was your first day."

"Yes, sir, no, sir, three bags full, sir," I said under my breath, and he laughed. "What can I do for you, sir? Let me know and I'll get to it right away."

"You're learning," he said. "I'm glad we're not going to have any issues. Remember you're the one that didn't want to discuss what happened this past weekend," he said softly. "I don't expect you to take out your girl issues on me."

"Say what?" My voice was loud. "What girl issues?"

"You know." He sighed. "The games that you girls play when you don't get your way. I know all about them. I have a sister that is the queen of miscommunication and immaturity."

"Are you calling me immature?"

"No," he said, his tone amused again. "I'm just saying if you have that girly immature bone in your body, don't try and use it on me. I'm immune after having grown up with Liv and Alice."

"I couldn't care less about playing any sort of games with you, Scott Taylor," I said, incensed at his comments; he was so darn rude. "I don't even know Liv and Alice in person, and I don't appreciate you comparing me to them."

"Aw, you don't like playing games?" he said, his voice husky.

"Nope," I said stiffly.

"Not even in the bedroom?" he said, his voice lowering. "Not even in my bed?"

"Whatever," I said, my stomach tingling with excitement as my brain wanted to scream, *Hell yeah, I want to play games with you in the bedroom!*

"Would you be saying 'whatever' if I told you I have this board game called 'Do It or Kiss It'?"

"Do It or Kiss It?" I said, curiosity making me ask more.

"You have to do what's on the card or kiss the body part that you choose from a bag."

"Oh, okay?"

"So yeah, you could go from taking your bra off to sucking my cock."

"Scott!" I said, my voice more shocked than it should have been as both tasks sounded pretty good right about then and I'd done both things with him already, "this is not appropriate."

"Am I making you blush?" he said, his tone low again as if he were trying to seduce me. "Or maybe not? I don't remember you blushing when I fucked you this past weekend."

"Really? 'Fucked' is the word you're going to use? Not 'made love' or 'had sex,' but 'fucked'? Typical man."

"I would say typical feminist, but I don't think you are one."

"Is there anything else I can do for you tonight, sir?" I said, changing the subject. I knew he was trying to rile me up and I wasn't going to let him do that to me.

"Call me sir again," he said. "And wear no panties to work tomorrow."

"You're so inappropriate," I said again as I debated in my mind the virtues of going panty-less to work, just to turn him on. I wanted to slap myself for even considering it.

"I'll see you tomorrow, Eliza."

"Goodbye, Scott."

"Good night," he said and then he hung up. I immediately face-timed Lacey again and squealed as she answered.

"What happened?" She frowned as she stared at me. "You had me on hold forever. I had to hang up."

"Scott called me," I said and stared into the phone.

"I know, you told me that when you put me on hold." The corners of her mouth turned up. "What did he have to say?"

"He wanted me to come over tonight," I said excitedly, though I wasn't sure why I was so giddy. "He said it was for work stuff, but then he started talking about sex and stuff, so I'm sure he was hoping for more."

"What sex stuff?"

"Sex games, girl."

"Sex games." Lacey's brown eyes looked into the phone with an excited and shocked expression. "What games? Oh shit, is he into kinky stuff?"

"I think he was talking about a board game, but who knows?" I said and laughed, my mind immediately wondering how kinky Scott was—and how kinky I would be, given the opportunity.

"Sure, he has a board game." She laughed. "That's what they all say. He totally wants you to go over there and suck on his balls."

"Lacey, you're gross."

"No, I'm just honest." She laughed. "I bet he wants you to suck on—"

"Lacey," I groaned. "Please do not continue with what you were going to say."

"Why not?" She giggled. "It's good for me to talk out my ideas for when I write my book, *Play the Player*."

"I thought you were joking about that."

"I was, at first," she said. "But now ... now I'm thinking that I'm going to write it."

"I thought you were writing a literary masterpiece, that was going to go on to win a Pulitzer and a Nobel Literature Prize?"

"Yeah, but maybe what I really need to write is a good old sexy book." She giggled. "And make some money and move out of my parents' house and move and live with you."

"I'm totally down for that." I grinned. "And that is a book I would want to read. It would be great."

"Hmm," she said. "Do you really think so?" Her voice was soft and I knew then that she wasn't just joking around. She was being 100% serious. And I have to admit that a part of me was excited as hell.

"I really think so." I nodded. "You could even self-publish it. You don't have to get an agent or anything. My friend Betsy-Sue—well, an online friend I met in a wanna-be actress forum—told me that her best friend is an author as well and that she self-publishes books and, girl, she made five thousand dollars last month."

"Five thousand dollars?" Lacey squealed. "Okay, sign me up!"

"But what about your other book? Your magnum opus?"

"I can write it later. You know I love romance and, honestly, after coming up with my 'play the player' title, I've been writing down some notes and stuff."

"Oh, really?" I smiled into the phone, suddenly happy and a bit curious as to when she'd made the notes. She'd only just told me about the idea in the first place. "Then yes, you can tell me ideas you have as you're writing the book, even those that include descriptions of sucking."

"And fucking?" She giggled.

"Don't use the term fucking. It's so unromantic." I frowned. "I just said that to Scott as well."

"You talked to him about fucking?" she said, her eyes wide and I wondered how she was going to write a filthy book if she was so shocked at everyday talk.

"Yes, he talked to me about it. I told him I preferred the term 'making love' or 'having sex.' Well, I kinda told him that."

"You did not." Lacey frowned. "Eliza!"

"What?"

"You sound like one of those wishy-washy girls." Lacey shook her head. "That is not how you play the player."

"I'm not playing him. You know my plan. Flirt casually, do the lap dance, embarrass him and peace out."

"But you could make this even more exciting." She giggled. "You could really give him a taste of his own medicine. It seems to me that he thinks you're up for the taking, anyway."

"He does, doesn't he?" I said and pursed my lips. "He thinks that just because I slept with him easily once, that it's going to happen again. He even told me to wear no panties to work tomorrow."

"Do it!" Lacey giggled.

"What?"

"Do it." She nodded knowledgably. "The last thing he expects you to do is to wear a skirt tomorrow with no panties. He was testing you. He is playing games with you. He will be shocked if you actually take control of the situation and do what he says."

"What?" I stared at her. "Are you joking or being serious?"

"I'm being totally serious." She nodded. "He thinks he has you where he wants you right now. And he's teasing and testing you, and he knows that he is in control. You need to gain that control back. You need to make him think about what he is saying and doing. You need him to take a step back and think, 'Shit, this girl is sexy. I want her. But I don't know if I can have her.'"

"But he's already had me."

"Yeah, but guys are dumb. It doesn't matter if he's had you every night for two years, as soon as he thinks he can't have you, he'll suddenly want you even more."

"Am I your test subject for your book?" I asked her with a giggle.

"No," she said, but she laughed. "I've decided not to write a full book, maybe I'll just release a novella first and see how that goes. If I think I'm going to become a hot romance author, then I'll expand it."

"That sounds like a good idea," I said and paused. "Will you still come here to write it?"

"Are you still willing to buy my flight?" she asked softly, and I nodded, beaming into the phone.

"Done." My voice expressed my extreme excitement. "I can't wait. When are you going to come?"

"Whenever you can get the flight." She grinned back at me. "I figure it will be easier for me to let my inner slut fly and write this book if I'm away from my parents. I don't need my dad walking into my room asking me to read a scene out loud and it's about some guy anally penetrating some girl for the first time."

"Lacey," I groaned, "you're going to write anal in a romance book?"

"I'm not talking Harlequin Presents, here, Eliza." She giggled. "I'm talking full-on sexy, 'let me go home to my husband and have him flip me over on the bed'—or 'bend me over the desk,' in your case."

"You need a life." I giggled. "And a husband."

"We both need husbands." She giggled. "Preferably millionaires, so we don't have to go and work our crummy jobs and can just concentrate on our crafts."

"Yeah, when you meet a millionaire, let me know." I laughed. "And by the way, we've just missed the first twenty minutes of *The Bachelor*."

"This is better than *The Bachelor*," Lacey said. "Dude, this is like 'date my boss,' or something."

"Well, not for me. Scott and I are not going to be dating. He's an asshole."

"Just see how it goes, Eliza. Maybe he has a good explanation."

"For why he told me he was going out of town, or for why he told me to wear no panties to work tomorrow?"

"Well, we know the answer to the latter." She giggled. "And that's all that matters."

"Yeah, I guess." I sank back onto the couch and groaned. "I just feel so annoyed at myself for even being interested in him still. I don't know why I can't shake that excited feeling from my stomach. I know he just wants sex, but a part of me doesn't care. A part of me wants to just give it to him and say to hell with it."

"I know," Lacey said. "But don't do it. You know you can't do sex without a relationship. You can tease him, but don't go too far."

"I know, but I've kinda already slept with him, Lacey. What does it matter now?" I said. "He's already hit it."

"I hate that term." Lacey frowned. "So crude."

"You're the porno writer." I grinned. "Get used to it, baby. Hit it and quit it."

"Yeah, I can see the sentence in my book now. 'Sir James Knight hit it and quit it before he anally penetrated her the next day.'"

"Ewww," I laughed. "Also, is that technically possible? If he hit it and quit it, how can he be returning the next day for anal? Doesn't 'hit it and quit it' mean he never came back for more?"

"Ha ha, I guess you're right." Lacey laughed. "I guess the hitting it can be the anal."

"Enough with the anal, already," I groaned. "You've never even had anal. Why would you want to write about it?"

"I dunno." She laughed, and I could see her yawning as she lay back in the bed. "Seems more exciting than wham, bam, thank you, ma'am."

"Are you going to research?" I asked her lightly, watching her face go red. "Are you going to look for a man to show you all these things?"

"Yeah, right." Lacey rolled her eyes as she continued to blush. For all her talk, Lacey was even more innocent than me. I knew for a fact that Lacey had never had a one-night stand, and I knew for a fact that Lacey wasn't the sort to go to work with no panties. She was truly all-talk and no action. Unlike me. I could talk the talk and walk the walk.

"I'm going to find you a good guy when you get here."

"You can't even find a good guy for yourself." She laughed, and I joined her, allowing the laughter to rack my body as I sank into the couch and groaned.

"Well, we'll both find good guys," I said. "There has to be someone that can appreciate both of us."

"Not the same guy, please," Lacey said. "You know I love you, but I don't want to share the same man with you."

"Ha ha, idiot. Of course, two separate guys. Maybe two best friends? That would be cool."

"Yeah, that would be really cool," she agreed. "Work on it." Then she yawned again. "Okay, I'm going to sleep now. Call me tomorrow and give me an update."

"Will do."

"And don't forget."

"Forget what?"

"No panties." She giggled. "He asked for it, and I'm betting he'll be shocked when he realizes that you went through with it."

"Yeah, he'll be shocked alright," I said as I hung up the phone. I sat back on the couch and thought about what Lacey had said. She was correct in what she'd said. Scott had been teasing me when he'd said no panties. Teasing me and riling me up. I'd show him. I'd show him that I wasn't a girl to be intimidated. I wasn't going to wear panties and I was going to let him know in a way that would leave him speechless. That would teach *him* to play games with me. That would show *him* that I, Elizabeth Jeffries, was no 'wishy-washy' girl, as Laccy had put it.

Chapter Eight

Some women are born with sex appeal. They own their power over men and they flaunt it. There are some women that know that there is no barrier to turning a man on. You can be any size, any race, any religion; none of that matters when it comes to sex appeal. If you're a confident woman and you know how to work what you've got, then you can turn on any man.

Unfortunately, I'm not one of those women. I know that I'm attractive, but I also know I'm not Angelina Jolie or Halle Berry. I don't wake up in the morning looking like a million bucks. I also don't have men eating out of the palm of my hand, and I've tried more than a couple of times to seduce unsuspecting men. It just hasn't worked out well for me. Not in high school when I went after a guy on the football team (granted, he turned out to be gay), not in college when I tried to make out with a guy (granted, we kissed and I think it could have gone further if he hadn't suddenly recognized me as being a student in his class—hey, I see nothing wrong with professor-student relationships) and definitely not in my post-college life—jeez, I was on a dating website going out with guys like Bubba, for heaven's sake. So it was with trepidation that I made my way into the office with my short skirt and no panties. I was quite sure that I'd lost my mind as I walked. I could feel the cool air between my legs and there was a stirring in my stomach that told me that a part of my body thought this whole idea was tantalizing. That was the part of my body that I wanted to disown for being a kinky bitch, though secretly I loved her.

"Good morning, Elizabeth." Scott was waiting next to my desk as I walked into the room. My eyes immediately flew to his, and I smiled widely at him before I remembered that he wasn't someone I wanted to give the time of day to anymore.

"Oh, good morning," I said and looked away from him. My hands flew to my skirt and I flattened it and tried to pull it down as much as I could. I looked down and saw the hem ending at the middle of my thighs and I wondered what I'd been thinking going out looking like I was on my way to the club.

"Is this your first time working in an office?" he asked as he looked down at my long bare legs. It was then that I realized that I'd forgotten to put on my pantyhose. And I'd spent a good twenty minutes looking for a pair without runs as well!

"Excuse me? Why would you ask that?" I asked him defensively. Was it that obvious I wasn't used to a business environment?

"Your outfit," he said with a raised eyebrow as he looked down at my skirt. "Not that I'm complaining, but that's not a typical outfit most assistants and secretaries would wear."

"I see," I said with pursed lips. I have to admit that I wasn't that upset at his comment; more embarrassed. I mean, let's be realistic, most professional office workers aren't wearing short skirts to work.

"Don't tell me I've offended you?" he asked, his lips curled up in a cross between a grin and a snarl. He reminded me of an observant wolf waiting for his time to jump.

"Why would I be offended?" I looked him in the eyes. "I can't help it if I'm a sexy bitch." I licked my lips slowly and my eyes fell to his crotch and then looked back up. I could see the shock in his eyes as I smiled coyly. I wasn't an actress for nothing. I knew how to make men like him squirm, even if it didn't come naturally to me. As long as I pretended it was just a role, I could do just about anything. I grinned to myself as his shocked look became confused and perplexed. He didn't know what was going on. I'd gone from offended and slightly shy to confident and assertive in half a second. He was probably wondering if I had some sort of split personality. I was even wondering where it had come from. Actually, that's a lie. I knew where it came from. It came from deep inside of me. It came from the part of myself that I wish I were brave enough to let out more often. I was that girl. I didn't take shit, but sometimes I wasn't brave enough to speak up.

"Yes, you are," he said and nodded after a couple of seconds. "Sexy, I mean, not a bitch." He fumbled his words slightly, and I wanted to ask him if I'd taken him aback. Maybe he didn't know women as well as he thought he did. Maybe his sister Liv and her best friend Alice didn't have this side to their personalities.

"So are we ready to work, then?" I unbuttoned the top button of my shirt and shook my hair back casually. I loved being in control of the situation. I loved watching him squirm. My fingers fell to the second button on my shirt, and I could see that Scott's eyes were ready to pop out of his face.

"Yes, let's go into my office," he said finally, and I could see him swallowing. It made me feel with giddy with power. I was having this amazing sexual effect on him.

"Hold on," I said softly and reached over and brushed the front of his shirt, allowing my fingers to rub along his chest for a good few seconds. I stared up into his eyes and licked my lips as I let my hair fall forward across my face. "You had some fluff on your shirt," I said softly as I gazed up into his mesmerizing blue eyes. I was about to move back when I felt his hands clasp behind my waist and pull me into him even closer. His hands fell down my back and smoothed down the back of my skirt, as his fingers ran across my ass. I gasped as I felt him squeezing my butt and his eyes laughed at me.

"You had some fluff on your butt," he said with a wink, and we stood there just staring at each other as our bodies pressed against each other lightly.

"How could you see fluff on my butt?" I asked him softly, barely able to breathe as my breasts pressed against his chest.

"The same way I can see that you have no panties on." He leaned forward and whispered in my ear. "I just knew."

"I have panties on." I swallowed hard as I felt something moving against my stomach. Scott was growing hard, and I was no longer in control of the situation. I was still loving the situation, but I was no longer in charge. And I didn't really care either.

"Liar," he said gently and I felt his lips on my cheek, pressing gently against my skin. I moaned slightly and breathed him in, melting deeper into him. He smelled sexy and zesty and masculine, and I leaned forward and breathed him in again. "Noir by Tom Ford," he said.

"What?" I asked, my face turning red.

"My cologne. You like the smell, right?"

"I, uh, I didn't say that."

"You didn't have to say it. Haven't you realized by now, Elizabeth?"

"Realized what?" I was feeling flustered now.

"That I can read minds and I have eyes in the back of my head." He finally let me go and stepped back. "Though I wouldn't mind making sure."

"Making sure what?" I said. "You mean double checking what cologne you have on today?"

"No." He smiled, his eyes darkening. "That's not what I want to check."

"What is it you want to check?"

"If you have on any panties, of course."

"Pig," I said and turned around. I thought the no-panties idea was meant to take him by surprise. I thought he would be shocked that I'd come into work commando.

"I asked you. I didn't think you would do it." He came up behind me and I felt his hands sliding up over my shirt and cupping my breasts.

"What are you doing?" I said without moving. His hands were warm as his fingers pinched my nipples and cupped my breasts firmly in his palms.

"Seeing if you're braless as well."

"I'm not braless," I said, and I could feel my nipples getting hard from his touch.

"Pity." He groaned, his breath warm next to my neck as he spoke.

"Scott," I said as his right hand slid down my shirt and his fingers slowly pushed down into my skirt. "Scott!" I said louder as his hand made its way further down.

"Yes?" he said, as his fingers confirmed that I wasn't wearing any panties.

"You can't do that," I moaned, though I was anxiously awaiting his next move. Was he going to slip his fingers between my legs?

"I already have," he grunted, as one finger pressed against the inside of me firmly. I felt him moving it back and forth and it rubbed my wet bud slightly.

"Scott," I groaned and grabbed his arm and pulled his hand out of my skirt. "What are you doing?" I pulled away from him and took a deep breath. I felt hot and bothered and I knew that I was absolutely not in control of this situation at all.

"I'll make a deal with you," he said with a smile as I turned to look at him.

"What's the deal?" I asked him suspiciously.

"I'm going to ask you one question." He glanced at my heaving breasts and grinned. "And it's a question you should know the answer to."

"Okay ... and?"

"If you get the answer right, I will play by your rules the rest of the day." His eyes pierced mine. "However, if you get the answer wrong, you will play by my rules."

"What are your rules?" I asked him, with narrowed eyes.

"You'll see if I win."

"Hmm." I frowned. "I don't know. If I should know the answer, why would you even think you have a shot?"

"Call it intuition." He grinned.

"Fine," I said, my hands on my hips. I'd win and then he would have to play by my rules. That would show him. Though, I have to admit a part of me was curious what he would do if I got the question wrong. What would he want? What would he have up his sleeve? My stomach curled just thinking about it. My legs were still tingling from his intimate touch against my body. I could feel a heat between my legs that told me that I very much wanted to know what he would want.

"Okay, here goes." He stepped back and grinned. "Here's the question."

"Come on," I groaned. "Stop dragging it out. And don't make it some crazy science or math question and say I should have learned it in high school."

"It's not a hard question." He smiled. "All you have to do is tell me what I do."

"What?" My face froze as I stared at him. My heart started beating fast and I could feel my stomach flipping. Shit! I didn't know what he did.

"It's a simple question." He smiled. "And you do work here now, so one would assume you'd know the answer."

"Well, duh, of course I know. What a stupid question," I said, glaring at him in a haughty manner. "Now give me a serious question."

"No, I think this is fine," he said smugly. "What do I do for a living? I mean, it's an easy question, Elizabeth. You're my assistant. How could you not know?"

"I, uh, you're the manager."

"Manager of what?"

"Manager of me, duh." I tossed my hair. "Now I win. And my rules are that you do not touch me in the office. It's inappropriate."

"Actually, no, you haven't answered the question, so you don't win, but before we get back to that, what do you mean I can't touch you in the office? Can I touch you out of the office?"

"No," I squeaked out loudly. "I mean, let's just keep this relationship professional."

"Even though we've already had sex?"

"It was once." I licked my lips. "We can forget about that instance."

"It was more than once." He stepped toward me. "In fact, if I remember correctly, it was more like five times."

"It was one occasion," I said and took a step back.

"Well, it was two days technically. Seeing as we had sex in the night and the morning."

"Scott!" I hissed.

"I'm just trying to be technically accurate. I can't forget one instance when it was more than one instance."

"Whatever." I rolled my eyes, but all this talking about our multiple instances was reminding me of how good those instances were. And I didn't want to think about that right now.

"True, it is a 'whatever' moment." He grinned. "Because you lost and I won."

"I did not lose."

"What do I do?" His eyes bore into mine. "Tell me, what is my job? Or even what does our company do?"

"You are a manager and I am your secretary. And you have a secretary because you have an important enough job." Frigging A, even I knew I sounded pathetic. I couldn't believe that I'd spent so much time focused on Scott that I hadn't bothered to read up on the job he actually did.

"So you knew I was an accountant?" he asked.

"I was just about to say that!" I cried out. "I was just going to say you're the best accountant here and that I was hired to help you because I'm good with numbers."

"I'm not an accountant, Elizabeth." He grinned. "I'm an account manager for a board game company."

"I knew that," I said, but inside I was wondering if he was lying again. A board game company?

"Sure you did." He shook his head. "You got this job through a temp agency, didn't you?"

"How did you know?" I lied, thanking God he didn't know the truth. Though, it suddenly hit me that I wasn't sure how I'd actually gained access to the company. How had this Helen Smith gotten me this job?

"You're an actress, right?" He looked confident and smug as he spoke. "I guess you needed some extra money while waiting for an acting gig."

"Yeah." I nodded. Of course he was right, I did need extra money while waiting for acting gigs, but I wasn't temping. I had sold my soul to Candy Canes Birthday Grams so I could pay the bills while trying to find a long-term acting job. Candy Canes paid the bills, but I was increasingly feeling like I had sold out. Maybe temping would have been better. At least I wouldn't have found myself in situations like this: pretending to be a secretary to some sexy guy I'd slept with so that I could give him a lap dance and embarrass him at work. The more I thought about it, the less innocent and harmless it felt. Even if he was a jerk. I really didn't like lying, and I was starting to feel like perhaps I was no better than Scott. Maybe I'd overreacted to his lie. I mean, it had only been a hookup. He didn't owe me anything.

"Come into the office and lock the door behind you," he said, interrupting me from my thoughts.

"What?" I frowned and blinked up at him.

"My rules. You lost." He winked. "Come into my office and lock the door behind you."

"What are you going to do?"

"You'll see." He grinned and then turned around and walked into his office. I stood there staring at his back and my stomach curled in excitement. Were we about to have office sex? Oh gosh, why was I so excited at the possibility? Where had my resolve gone?

I was meant to be strong and in charge, but now, now I just wanted him to take me.

I took a couple of deep breaths before walking into Scott's office five steps behind him. I could hear other people talking in the building and I thought about what someone would have said if they'd walked in on him squeezing my breasts while his other hand was down my skirt. I would have been the one embarrassed then. I would have felt like a cheap whore. How would that have looked? Second day on the job and already letting my boss fondle me and openly enjoying it. I would have died of humiliation, though that didn't stop me from walking into his office feeling like a kid entering a candy store with a whole dollar in her pocket. I closed the door behind me and froze.

"There's no lock," I said, my throat dry as I stood there. It was completely obvious now that I expected something dirty to happen. I mean, why else would I care if the door locked?

"Come to the table." Scott motioned me toward him and I watched as he picked up a stack of files from the end of the table and dropped it on his chair. I swallowed hard as I waited for him to tell me to bend over and stick my ass in the air. "What are you thinking right now?" he asked me softly.

"If the air is going to be cold and if you're as kinky as James Spader," I said honestly.

"If the air is cold?" he asked softly with a smirk.

"On my ass," I said and made to bend over the desk.

"What are you doing?" he asked as he grabbed my arm.

"Getting into position."

"That's not the position I want you in." He shook his head and grinned.

"Oh," I said, disappointed.

"What did you mean by asking me if I was as kinky as James Spader?"

"Haven't you seen that movie *Secretary*?" I asked him, and he shook his head again, though his eyes looked interested.

"I should watch it, though, if that's a fantasy of yours."

"It's not a fantasy," I said and swallowed hard. Why had I mentioned James Spader? He wasn't someone that oozed sex appeal and the movie wasn't particularly sexy, either. However, there had been a few scenes that had left me breathless. There had been a few scenes where I'd sat back and wondered "What if that was me?"

"Sit on the desk," he said firmly as he suddenly changed the subject. I jumped up and leaned back and looked at him, waiting to see what was going to happen next.

"Lie back," he said, and I lay back and leaned my head against the desk. I wiggled around, trying to get comfortable, but the hardness of the wood never let up. "Close your eyes," he said, and I looked up at him instantly. "Can't you listen properly? I said close your eyes."

"Why?" I asked, my face growing warm.

"No questions. Just do it."

"Fine," I said and lay back, waiting. Nothing happened right away and I lay there listening to the sound of two people laughing. The sound was oddly soothing and I concentrated on that. My body jerked as I felt his hands on my legs and then on my skirt, casually pulling it up. I could feel myself growing wet as he lifted my ass up and left my bunched-up skirt there. I kept my eyes closed tightly the whole time, even as he spread my legs wide, pushing them as far apart as he could. I could feel the cool air between my legs and I shivered, wondering what was going to happen next. I heard a thump, but had no idea what it was. I was breathing heavier now as my stomach started to twirl. And then, just when I thought I could take the anticipation no more, I felt the tip of Scott's tongue on my throbbing clit, soft and tender as it licked back and forth. I moaned as I lay there and his tongue became longer as he flicked it against my clit.

"Oh!" I cried out as he started to suck on my clit, and I felt his hands holding my legs down as he devoured me. His tongue entered me and I could feel my juices streaming into his face as my body quaked against his mouth. He continued his movements eagerly, as if he were dining on a gourmet meal and wanted to enjoy every single bite. His tongue felt smooth and thick as it moved inside me, and I found myself screaming as he brought me to orgasm. I was sad as he pulled his tongue out of me, and I lay there waiting for him to enter me with his cock. I grabbed the sides of the table and waited to feel him enter me.

"Up now," he said and I looked up at him in confusion.

"What?" I said, flustered, as I sat up. He grabbed my arms and pulled me off of the table and carefully pulled my skirt down as I stood there in front of him.

"We're done." He licked his lips slowly and deliberately. "Now let's get to work. Have you played many board games before?" he asked as he sat down on his chair casually and opened his laptop. "Get your pen and paper, we have work to do."

✦ ✦ ✦

"What are you doing?" Scott said as soon as I answered the phone.

"Are you going to ask me that every time you call me?" I said as I sat back on my couch and paused the TV. I curled my legs up on the chair and leaned my head back.

"Perhaps," he said with a laugh. "By the way, I just watched *Secretary*."

"Oh?"

"The movie you recommended."

"I didn't recommend it."

"Are you into BDSM?"

"What?" I screeched.

"You compared me to James Spader's character. I can only think that's because you like a good spanking and think I would like giving it to you."

"I never said that."

"Is that what you want me to do?" His voice became husky. "Do you want me to bend you over my desk and spank you?"

"Of course not. Why are you calling me?"

"Why won't you let me explain about what happened last weekend?" he said with a sigh.

"It doesn't matter," I muttered.

"We should watch a movie together here," he said. "Maybe get in some neutral territory."

"I'm not watching *Secretary* with you," I said with a laugh.

"I just watched it," he said. "I don't need to watch it again. We can watch something else."

"Okay, good." I wasn't sure why I was agreeing to watch anything with him.

"Not that *Secretary* wasn't good. It's more intense than I thought it would be. Slightly sexy, but deeper than I thought."

"Yeah, the movie was more about how they fit into each other's lives than the lifestyle they enjoyed," I said as I remembered the movie. "He filled that need in her and she filled that need for him, though it was unconventional. They were lucky to find each other."

"Yes, I can't imagine most women would want to deal with an emotionally unavailable man."

"I wouldn't," I said.

"I can tell," he said. "Though you're the one that seems more closed off than I am."

"I'm not closed off," I said quickly.

"Yes, you are," he said softly. "I suppose it's not my place to say that, but you are. Did your ex-boyfriend hurt you?"

"Why are you calling me, Scott?" I said loudly, changing the subject.

"I just wanted to tell you I'd just watched *Secretary*."

"You could have told me that at work."

"I guess so. I guess I wanted to tell you before tomorrow. The movie really got me thinking."

"About what?"

"About us. About abuse of power. About if we're crossing some line that neither of us wants to acknowledge."

"You're the one crossing the line, Scott. You're the one that told me to get on your table and spread my legs."

"Did you regret it?" His voice was husky. "Did you regret coming on my face?"

"No," I said again. "I'm just saying that it's you crossing the line."

"I'm not a dominant, Elizabeth," he said. "If you want to have some fun with me from here on out, you can make the first move. Like tomorrow. Come to work and do what you want."

"I don't want to do anything."

"Liar," he said. "You know I have two sisters. I know how girls act when they don't want a guy."

"How?" I frowned into the phone.

"There's a nonchalance, an annoyed tone, an awkward dismissal. You don't have any of that toward me."

"I've dismissed you," I said. "Stop being so arrogant."

"I'm not arrogant, just right. Just remember you can come to work tomorrow and have your wicked way with me."

"Don't count on it," I said. "I'm coming to work to work," I lied. I was going to be happy when this week was over. Everything was getting way too complicated.

Chapter Nine

There was a large bouquet of mixed colorful flowers sitting on my desk when I walked into the office the next day. Bright pinks, oranges, yellows, greens and purples beamed up at me as I stared down at the different petals. I could feel my heart beating fast as Scott walked out of his office.

"Morning, Elizabeth," he said with a bright smile.

"Morning," I replied and cocked my head. "Are the flowers from you?"

"Yes," he said and walked toward me. "I wanted us to start fresh. I wanted to apologize for anything I've said or done that might have been offensive."

"Oh, really?" I knew I sounded surprised.

"Yes." He grinned. "I lied when I said I was going out of town last weekend. I'm sorry. I had my reasons, but that wasn't right."

"It's fine." I shrugged. "I don't care."

"It's not fine, but if you don't care …" His voice trailed off and I could see he looked unsure of himself. It made me feel bad for a few seconds, but I ignored the feeling. I didn't want Scott to redeem himself and humanize himself as more than a sexual object. It scared me. The fact of the matter was that I liked being alone. It was comfortable and safe. I liked that I could hate him while desiring him at the same time. It made it so that things couldn't get too deep. There could be no heartbreak if I didn't let him in deep enough to break it.

"I need you to come over and do some work tonight," he said and pulled out some keys from his pocket. "Come over around seven. I'm going to dinner, so I might be a little late, but make yourself at home. We're going to have a late night working. There's a board game conference next month and we're launching three new games, so I want to get some test groups set up."

"Okay." I nodded as I took the keys from him. "I'll be there."

"Good, let's get to work. I want to go over some numbers with you for a meeting tomorrow. I'm going to need you to give a presentation."

"Presentation? I haven't even been here a week."

"You can fake it." He grinned. "You're an actress, after all."

"I'm an actress of the 'Frankly, my dear, I don't give a damn' and 'To be or not to be' variety. Not the 'And when you land on Park Avenue, you have the opportunity to buy it or let it go to auction' variety."

"So you like Monopoly?" he asked with a grin. "We don't actually make that board game here. Hasbro is one of our biggest competitors, but I'll admit it's a good classic. You can come over and play it some time if you want to."

"I don't want to." I frowned.

"Or you can come to one of my family board game nights." He continued. "My family loves getting together and playing games."

"You guys must all be really close," I said, slightly envious. "You talk about your sister a lot."

"We're all quite close, particularly Aiden, Liv and I. My older brother Chett and my older sister Gabby keep more to themselves, but Liv, Aiden and I are really close." He nodded and smiled. "It's nice."

"You're really lucky," I said. "My family is quite dysfunctional."

"Oh, so is mine." He laughed. "Remember I told you about my sister and her boyfriend?"

"The guy you said was putting up with her crap?"

"Yeah." He grinned. "Well, he was kinda fake-dating my older sister Gabby when he started hooking up with Liv, only Liv didn't know."

"What?" I asked, my jaw falling open. "Are you serious?"

"Yup, he was kinda fake-engaged to Gabby."

"But he was dating Liv?" I said incredulously.

"Yup." He nodded. "They hooked up at some wedding."

"Wow." I stared at him in shock. "You're joking, right?"

"Nope." He laughed. "So, yeah my family is a bit crazy too."

"There has to be more to that story." I gazed at him curiously.

"There is." He nodded. "Maybe I can tell you over dinner sometime."

"I don't know." I bit my lower lip.

"No pressure." He shrugged. "I could also tell you in bed, if you'd prefer that."

"In bed?" I stared into his eyes.

"After we make love, but before we fall asleep." He grinned. "That's when most intimate talk happens, right?" His fingers brushed a loose tendril of hair behind my ear. "If you prefer that, we can make that happen."

"We're not going to be making love again." I stifled a groan.

"Okay," he said, and I frowned. Okay? That was it? "The next move is up to you, Elizabeth," he said softly and stepped back. "You already know what I want," he said and smiled at me. "Make yourself a coffee and come into my office in fifteen minutes. We have work to be doing."

"Yes, sir," I replied, slightly miffed.

"I can be your Sir, if you want," he said softly. "You just have to tell me what you want." He looked at my lips and then back up to my eyes. "I'm not James Spader, Elizabeth. I'm not going to command you to come into my office so I can spank you."

"You commanded me to come into your office the other day." I said, defensively.

"Because I won a bet." He grinned. "The next time you want me to make you orgasm, you're going to have to ask me for it."

"Well, you'll be waiting a long time for me to ask you for anything," I said in a huff as my stomach flipped at my words. Not only did my stomach flip at the thought of him going down on me again, but my breasts were starting to tingle and my brain was screaming at me that next time I was in that situation, I was to make sure that I felt him inside of me as well—and not just his tongue.

"We'll see." He grinned and walked back into his office. "Fifteen minutes, Elizabeth. I expect you in here in fifteen minutes." I watched him sauntering back into his office and then turned back to my flowers. I picked them up and smelled them. I closed my eyes and enjoyed the wonderfully vibrant and fresh smell. I set them back on the table and sighed. It had been a nice gesture for him to get me the flowers. I wasn't sure why he'd gotten them for me. I wasn't sure if he was being sincere. Did he really want to start over? And if so, why? What did he want from me? And how would he feel if he knew that I'd been lying to him as well? I walked out of the office and toward the kitchen so I could make a coffee for myself before the work day began. I couldn't stop myself from smiling as I made my coffee and toasted a bagel. I knew that I was only here for a week and that this wasn't my real job, but I was excited about the day ahead. I was excited that I got to work with Scott, and see him and smell him. I liked being around him. Even with all his innuendos. He somehow made my day feel brighter and more exciting. And the flowers, well, the flowers had been a really sweet gesture. I was happy. I realized as I walked back to the office that even though I was confused, I was happy. And I wasn't going to question it. I wasn't going to overthink it. I was just going to let it be. And whatever was going to happen was going to happen. I was just going to enjoy the day and our light flirtation and maybe after everything went down, we could eventually be friends. I knew that was a long shot for multiple reasons, but stranger things had happened.

✦ ✦ ✦

"Where are you?" Lacey asked when I called her from Scott's claw foot bathtub.

"You will never guess," I said as I ran my finger through the water and bubbles.

"Paris?" Lacey guessed, and I rolled my eyes.

"I just spoke to you three hours ago, how could I be in Paris already?"

"I don't know. Concorde? Time travel?"

"Time travel?" I laughed. "Uh huh!"

"So where are you, then?"

"Guess again," I said with a giggle.

"I don't know." She sighed. "I'm guessing not Hong Kong."

"Hong Kong?" I was exasperated. "Come on, Lacey."

"Elizabeth Jeffries, how on God's green earth am I supposed to know where you are?"

"I'm at Scott Taylor's house," I whispered. "And I'm currently soaking in his claw foot tub."

"What?" she screeched. "You slept with Scott Taylor again?"

"No." I rolled my eyes, even though I knew she couldn't see me. "What do you take me for?"

"The girl who wore no panties to work, put her boss's hand up her skirt and is now at his house and in his bathtub."

"I didn't put his hand up my skirt. He put his hand down my skirt. And you're the one that told me to wear no panties in the first place, Lacey."

"I know, but I didn't mean for that to lead straight to his bed again."

"He's not even here yet." I muttered. "We didn't have sex. I'm just having a bath because I saw the claw foot tub and wanted to relax in some bubbles for a little bit, and he left a note saying he won't be back for another hour."

"Do you know how crazy that sounds, Eliza?" Lacey sounded perplexed. "You went to your boss's house to work and instead you're having a bath."

"I'm going to work after my bath. It's huge, Lacey. Like so huge that I can stretch out my whole body. You know how much I love baths!"

"Yes, I know you like baths, but that doesn't explain why you're currently in your boss's bath. What if he comes home and catches you?"

"I didn't think about that," I said and sighed into the phone. That was a lie, of course. I'd thought about it and dismissed it. He was going to be gone for an hour and I wouldn't take that long. Plus, if he did come back earlier, maybe he'd be so aroused that he'd make a move. Not that I wanted him to make a move, of course ... well, not really.

"If he sees you naked in his bath, he's going to think that that's an invitation to get into the bathtub and get naked with you."

"No, he won't," I said and sat up quickly in the bathtub and listened to see if I could hear any noises in the house. My heart was racing as I imagined him walking in and seeing my naked body covered by bubbles. What would he do? More than just go down on me, I was sure. He'd have to take me then. He wouldn't be able to resist me.

"Unless that's what you're hoping for," Lacey said, and I could tell what she was thinking because Lacey always knew what I was thinking.

"That's not what I'm hoping for," I protested as I looked at the fluffy white towel I'd taken out of Scott's linen closet. I debated getting out of the bath right then or allowing myself to soak in the bubbles and Epsom salts for a few more minutes.

"Sure, it's not." Lacey laughed. "You can fool Scott and you can even try to fool yourself, but you can't fool me."

"I'm not trying to fool anyone. I don't want to have sex with Scott Taylor again. He's a liar and he used me for a one-night stand." I repeated the words that had been running through my head all week. I had to keep reminding myself why I didn't want to get any more involved with him.

"Maybe you're being too hard on him, Eliza," Lacey said softly. "You haven't even given him a chance to explain."

"He lied," I said, though a part of me wondered if she wasn't right. Maybe I should give him a chance to explain. "You know how I feel about men that lie."

"He's not your dad," Lacey said. "Don't judge him based on what your dad did."

"I know," I said, my heart lurching. "I just don't like it when guys lie."

"I know you don't," she said, her voice compassionate. "But one lie doesn't mean he's a bad guy. It doesn't mean he's going to let you down. It doesn't mean that he's going to hurt you."

"But it could," I said. "It could mean that." My throat caught as I thought about Scott. "I wish I was stronger, Lacey. I wish I could give him a chance, but after my dad and Shane, well, I just can't go through that again."

"I know."

"It was too painful." My voice was raw as I mentioned my dad and my ex-boyfriend. All of a sudden I felt cold in the bath, even though the water was still warm. I felt empty inside as I sat there thinking about old hurts and heartaches. I felt empty and lost. What *was* I doing here sitting in Scott's bathtub? Hadn't I learned from my past mistakes? Why was I putting myself in this position to be hurt and rejected again? Just because of some good sex?

"I know," she said again and she did. She was the only one that really knew. She was the only one that had seen me cry: big, gut-wrenching, heartbreaking tears. She was the one that had seen me breaking down, the only one that had ever seen me break down. It had been right when I'd found out my boyfriend Shane was cheating on me. That alone hadn't caused me to break down. It had been the knowledge that my father, the one who had walked away from my mother and I when

I was only two, had walked his stepdaughter down the aisle. He didn't even know that I knew. He didn't know that I stalked him and his family to see what he was doing. I didn't even know why I cared. He wasn't in my life. Not even a little bit. I'd tried to see him when I was younger, but he'd always had an excuse at the last moment. He'd always had a reason why he couldn't come get me, and then we'd just stopped making plans and he'd faded out if my life. But when I'd gotten older, I'd looked for him. I'd been oddly unaffected when I'd realized he'd remarried and had stepkids. It didn't seem real. The pain never really surfaced. And then I'd seen a photo of him giving his stepdaughter away at her wedding, the day after I'd found out Shane was cheating on me, and I'd just lost it. My heart had broken into a million pieces. I'd completely lost it and I'd hit the walls in pain and anger, and that was when Lacey had walked in. She hadn't said a thing. Instead she'd put her arms around me and held me close to her. She'd let me cry until I couldn't cry anymore. She'd told me I was worthy of love and that she'd always love me. She'd told me I was her sister and best friend. She'd told me that it was my father's loss and I'd held onto those words, clutching them tightly to my soul when I felt down. I'd gotten over that moment, but the pain still existed in my heart. I always wondered why I hadn't been loved. Why my father had walked away so easily. Why he'd lied so many times when he'd said he was going to come pick me up. I wondered why Shane had cheated on me. Why he'd fallen for someone else. And now, anytime someone got too close and I thought they had the potential to hurt me, I backed away. It was an unconscious reaction, but I didn't know how to stop. I didn't know how to not overreact in these situations. I didn't know how to preserve my heart and still give someone a chance.

"You think I'm being too hard on Scott, don't you?" I stared at the bubbles in front of me as they ebbed back and forth.

"You're just doing the job you've been paid to do. I don't know that Scott deserves it, but it's not you that hired yourself," she said, but I knew what she was thinking.

"I know all guys aren't the same, Lacey. But he hasn't given me any reason to trust him." Though he had apologized and given me flowers. That should count for something, right? And it wasn't even that big a lie. Wasn't I technically the biggest liar in this situation?

"Maybe he had a good reason for his lie," she said. "I mean, what exactly do we know about this Helen person that hired you?"

"We know she's his ex, or something like that." I sighed. "I'm so confused."

"And that's okay, understandable even. You're confused because the situation is complicated. I just want you to really think everything through."

"You think he deserves a second chance?"

"No, I think you do. You like him, Eliza. And it's about more than just being sexually attracted to him. You like his personality. You like who he is as a man."

"He seems really close with his family," I said. "That makes me like him, you know. He talks about his sister a lot. I guess he really loves her. That's a good sign when someone is close to their family."

"He seems like he could be a good guy," Lacey said. "Give him a chance. I mean, you barely know him. Yes, you slept with him, but you don't really know him. Maybe you'll really like him and maybe you won't. But don't go ruining something before it even gets started. Don't go pushing him off when you know you like him."

"Well, I know I like sex with him." I giggled, feeling light-hearted again. "He's good in bed."

"Oh, Eliza." Lacey laughed. "Just give him and the situation a chance."

"So what do I do?" I sighed, knowing she was right. I couldn't keep running from situations that I thought might make me emotionally vulnerable. "The fact is, I'm there for a different reason. What do I do about the job I was hired for originally?"

"Do the job and maybe just don't give him a lap dance in front of anyone. Maybe tell him what you were hired to do, but ask him to not let anyone know you told him."

"So you think I should admit to him that this was an acting job?" I groaned. "It feels so duplicitous and cheap, almost. Like what sort of loser am I that these are the acting jobs I take? No Shakespeare or Broadway for me. No, siree. I work for a candy gram company, and my jobs are getting shadier and shadier every week."

"Let him know you studied acting in college. Let him know you're just doing this job with Candy Canes for the money. Tell him when you took the job, it was only supposed to be an acting job. That you're only working there to pay the bills until your big break."

"What if he thinks I slept with him to pay the bills? What if he thinks that—"

"Elizabeth, you're overthinking everything." Lacey laughed. "Stop and see what happens."

"You really think I should?"

"I think you want to," she said. "You went to work yesterday with no panties on and allowed him to go down on you, and today you're having a bath at his house. I'm not trying to be clever here, but let's be real—you want him. Badly."

"You were the one that told me to wear no panties." I blushed.

"Yeah, but not to let him go down on you at the office."

"That wasn't my plan." I giggled. "I just didn't know how to say no."

"Uh huh," Lacey drawled. "And you just happen to be having a bath right now because you just had to bathe your skin at this very moment. You're not hoping he'll come home and catch you in his bath tub, naked, right?"

"Lacey," I said as my face blushed. "Of course not."

"Uh huh. You can't fool me, Elizabeth Jeffries."

"Lacey," I groaned. "Stop it."

"Stop what?" She started laughing. "You totally want him to take you, but you wanted it to be one of those 'oh, I couldn't say no' situations."

"Shh," I groaned. "I'm that obvious, huh? He didn't even try anything at the office today. He says that he wants me to make the move if I want him. Come on now. I want to be ravished and taken." I giggled. "I want him to grab me and bend me over and have his wicked way with me because he just can't stop himself."

"I'm sure he wanted to." She laughed again. "I'm sure he was hoping you'd return yesterday's favor to him this morning."

"Lacey, stop it." I giggled. "There is no way he thought I was going to go down on him in the office." I shook my head. "Could you just imagine?"

"You're totally loving this, aren't you?" She laughed.

"Kinda," I admitted. "I'm confused about my feelings, but I'm enjoying the game, yes. Argh, what is my problem?"

"You like a guy and don't know if he's a dog or not." She laughed. "We all have that problem. Every single one of us. I don't know any single woman that doesn't wonder if the guy she met is a dog."

"Why is dating so hard?" I sighed. "And fake dating is even worse. And I'm not even really fake dating. This is such a mess. And so hard to figure out."

"It doesn't have to be hard. Well, that's preferable, but it can start off soft." Lacey giggled, and I rolled my eyes at her pun.

"Yeah, soft can get hard real quick," I said seriously, though I ruined it with a giggle. "Especially when I'm around."

"When you're around, the guys can't even control it," Lacey said. "It gets hard whether they want it to it not."

"I'm just that desirable," I said and laughed, feeling light and happy all of a sudden. "What would I do without you, Lacey?"

"Um, continue making men hard?" she asked and we both laughed. "And maybe continue taking naked baths in the home of your boss when you're supposed to be working."

"Oh, shit." I froze as I heard a door slamming. "I think he's home early, Lacey. What am I going to do?"

"Well, you have two choices." She giggled. "Hurry out of the bath and get dressed. Or hurry out of the bath and go into full-on seduction mode."

"What do you suggest I do?" I asked, my nerves on high as I heard Scott calling out my name.

"You know exactly what I'm going to suggest," Lacey said. "I'm going to suggest you do the same thing you're planning on doing."

"Oh God, Lacey. Am I crazy?" I groaned as I stepped out of the bathtub and picked up the fluffy white towel and wrapped it around my body.

"Not at all." She laughed. "Go for it, girl. Just don't let your doubts make you nervous."

"I wish I had a drink," I groaned as I stood there trying to gain up the courage to walk out of the door. "I need some liquid courage right now."

"No, you don't," Lacey said. "Go and have some fun. Go and rock his world."

"I'm going." I said and then hung up. I walked out of the bathroom at the same time that Scott reached the top of the stairs. He looked over at me with a surprised look, and I saw his eyes reviewing my body eagerly.

"Elizabeth?" he said as he walked over to me with questioning eyes. "What's going on?"

"You said the next move was mine, right?" I said and walked towards him. "Well, I'm ready to play, big boy. Are you?" I stopped in front of him and dropped the towel on the floor. Scott's eyes widened as he stared at my naked body, and I put my hand on my hip and tilted my face in a seductive pose.

"What's your move?" I said as I walked towards him and pressed my body into his. His body felt warm next to mine and I could feel my body shivering against his as I waited for him to speak.

"Scott, where are you?" I heard a female voice from down the stairs, and I froze for a second before grabbing my towel and running back to the bathroom, my face fire-engine red.

"Elizabeth, wait," Scott said and grabbed my hand. He pushed me back against the wall and his lips pressed down onto mine firmly. He kissed me for a few seconds as his fingers played with my breasts and I moaned against him. "Go into the bathroom and wait," he said as he pulled away from me, his eyes dark and mysterious.

"Who's downstairs?" I questioned him, wanting to know who he'd brought back with him.

"Go into the bathroom, turn the light off, bend over the bathtub and wait for me," he barked, not answering my question.

"But …" I started, but stopped as his eyes narrowed.

"Go," he said, a slight twinkle in his eye. I turned around and walked back to the bathroom quickly. As I walked away, I felt his hand slapping my bottom and I turned to look at him.

"What was that for?"

"Not listening," he said with a smile. "Now go into the bathroom and wait. I'll be there in a minute."

"Okay, James Spader—I mean, Scott Taylor," I said with a laugh and ran to the bathroom quickly as he shook his hand at me. I hurried into the bathroom and turned off the light and waited. My whole body was on fire, burning in anticipation for what was going to happen next. I bent over the bathtub and waited, my eyes closed and my ass tingling. And then I heard the door open and I almost jumped in excitement.

"Are you ready to play, Elizabeth Jeffries?" Scott's voice was deep and husky. "I'd like to teach you a new game."

Chapter Ten

"What new game?" I gasped as I felt Scott grabbing my hips and pulling me back towards him.

"You'll see." He laughed and I heard him undoing his zipper.

"Who was the girl downstairs?" I asked softly, as my body trembled.

"My sister, Liv," he said, his voice husky. "We had dinner, and I wanted her to meet you, but I guess you had other plans."

"Oh, I didn't realize," I said and froze as I felt him leaning over me. "What are you doing?"

"I'm turning the water on," he said as he turned the faucet on.

"Why?"

"You'll see." His fingers slid up to my breasts. "I didn't know I was going to come home to a surprise."

"Well, aren't you a lucky boy, then?"

"Yes," he said, his voice husky.

"So where did Liv go?" I asked softly, slightly sad that I wasn't getting to meet her. I was curious what his family was like. I wasn't sure why, as it didn't really matter.

"Home." He laughed. "She was annoyed with me because my brother Aiden likes her best friend, Alice, and she thinks that somehow I'm interfering in their relationship."

"Oh, how?" I gasped as he cupped my sex and ran his fingers between my legs.

"Because Alice and I kissed," he said gruffly as he played with me.

"Kissed?" I moaned as my body shook. A small dart of irrational jealousy ran through me at the thought of him kissing someone else.

"Yeah, it was nothing. Totally innocent. A quick kiss, late one night, but apparently Aiden is all bent out of shape about it. Like he thinks I want her. Which I don't. Not that she isn't great. I love her like a sister, but everyone knows that Aiden and Alice are meant to be together. They've both had a secret crush on each other for years. They just need to get together already."

"So you know your brother likes a girl, yet you still kissed her? You're right. Your family is dysfunctional."

"I didn't kiss her because I wanted her. I kissed her to get my brother to act. Now shh," he said as he removed his hand. "Get into the bath."

"What?" I said, confused. "I just had a bath."

"You just had a bath?" he sounded confused now.

"Don't worry about it," I said quickly and stepped into the tub. "It's a bit hot."

"You'll get used to it," he said. "Lay back."

"Oh, okay," I said and lay back. I could barely make out the outline of his face and I wondered if he was going to join me. "I thought I was the one in charge now?"

"No." He laughed. "I never said you were in charge. I said the next time you wanted something, you should make the first move."

"So you like to be in charge, huh?" I asked him softly as the water started to cover my body again.

"I don't mind, but I have a feeling that you like me to be in charge."

"I'm not sure why you think that," I said and gasped as I felt his fingers splashing water over my body and then his palms lightly rubbing my nipples.

"I don't think, I know," he said and stepped back. I could hear him taking his clothes off. "What a pleasant end to the evening."

"You would say that," I said with a smile. "This wasn't my plan when I came over, you know."

"Of course it wasn't."

"It wasn't!"

"And I'm saying of course it wasn't. You came over to work."

"Oh, shoot!" I exclaimed. "Should we get some work done first?"

"It can wait." He laughed. "I'm in no rush."

"I feel bad. Don't we have that big conference next week?" My voice trailed off as I spoke. I wasn't going to be at the conference next week, because my assignment would be over by then.

"We can talk about it later, or in the morning." He laughed. "Don't worry about it. I'm the boss. I make the decisions."

"Yes, sir." I made a face at him in the dark.

"I think you like that, don't you?" he said.

"Like what?"

"Having someone be in control. Have someone dominating you. Having someone be your Sir."

"No, I don't. That's never been something I've fantasized about," I said softly.

"You like being spanked, though." He growled. "You like being taken."

"No," I lied. I was still feeling turned on from the feel of his hand on my ass. "That's not something I've ever been into." Which was true; I'd never had a guy spank me before.

"I can't say I've ever done anything like that either," he said. "However, that movie got me to thinking."

"Thinking what?"

"That experimentation could be fun."

"You're not experimenting with me!"

"Why not?"

"Because you don't know me, and I'm your assistant!"

"You know how ironic your comment is, right?" He laughed. "I don't know you well enough to experiment with you, yet you're sitting in my bathtub, naked, waiting for me to fuck you."

"You're so crude." I blushed. "I was just trying to be adventurous. I wanted to have some fun."

"There's nothing wrong with that. I see nothing wrong with a woman allowing her sexual urges to lead her."

"I'm not letting my sexual urges lead me anywhere."

"They lead you to my bed the first night you met me."

"Are you calling me easy?"

"Not unless you're calling me easy." He laughed.

"I know everyone says this, but I'm not really a one-night stand girl. I'm not the girl that jumps into bed with every hot guy she meets."

"I don't care if you are. I don't judge," he said softly. "I'm not one of those guys. Whatever a man can do, a woman can do. And they should both be judged on who they are."

"I guess that's one plus of you having a sister," I said softly, pleased at his words. "You're more enlightened than most men."

"Yeah, you have Liv to thank for that." He laughed. "She's put me in my place many a time."

"I wish I could have met her."

"Next time."

"Yeah," I said and held in a sigh.

"Okay, my clothes are off and I'm coming in," he said, and I felt his leg next to mine as he stepped into the tub.

"We're going to have a bath together?" I laughed.

"No." He laughed and he leaned down and grabbed my hands. "Stand up."

"Oh?"

"Just do as I say," he said as he pulled me towards him. My wet body was slick over his dry one and my breasts crushed into his chest, slipping and sliding across his chest hair. "I want you to stand still."

"Stand still?"

"You like to repeat what I say a lot, don't you?"

"I'm just trying to figure out what's going on."

"You'll see soon enough."

"So you're single?" I said and Scott stilled at my words. I could feel my stomach dropping at the silence that fell in the room as we stood there.

"What sort of question is that?" he said finally.

"I'm just trying to make sure that we're both single here," I said quietly, my heart racing.

"I would certainly hope we're both single," he said as he squeezed my butt, his fingers cupping my butt cheeks as he moved in closer to me. I could feel his cock hanging and brushing against my stomach.

"I just want to make sure," I said. I wanted to ask him who Helen was. I wanted to ask him so badly, but didn't want him to ask how I knew about Helen in the first place.

"Step out of the bathtub," he growled, and I felt him step back from me.

"What?" His abrupt movement left my body cold.

"Out," he said, and he got out of the bathtub. I followed after him, wondering what was going on. "Lean forward like you were before." He said as he pushed me forward. "Hold on to the side of the tub."

"Shouldn't I dry off first?"

"No," he said and I felt him coming up behind me. I felt the tip of his cock rubbing against my clit and I moaned.

"Scott?" I said as I wiggled against him.

"Shh," he said and he stepped back, his cock falling from between my legs. "No questions," he said and I felt his hand slapping my ass lightly.

"Why not?" I squeaked out.

"That was another question," he said, slapping my ass again. This time it was a little hard and I could feel a light sting.

"You really like this slapping thing now, huh?"

"And another," he said and slapped again. This time it was a little harder, and I felt his fingers slip between my legs as he pulled his hand away.

"Okay, James," I moaned as I felt myself growing even wetter than before.

"It's Scott," he said as he rubbed his palms across my butt cheeks. "You might think this is some sort of role play, where I'm James Spader and you're Maggie Gyllenhaal from *Secretary*, but this is no role play."

"I don't remember him spanking her in a dark bathroom, so I never thought that," I said softly.

"You're just like her, though, aren't you? You want this badly." He growled as he pulled my ass back and pushed his hard cock between my legs. "You get off on me touching you in the dark, spanking you, rubbing you, fucking you."

"You haven't done much yet," I groaned, waiting in sweet anticipation as I felt the tip of his cock next to my entrance. "You're just a tease."

"I'll show you a tease," he grunted, and I felt him sliding inside of me. I felt my hands going weak as I leaned into the bathtub and I could hear myself crying out as his cock moved faster in and out of me. "I'm not a tease now, am I?"

"No," I moaned as my eyes flittered in my head. "Not at all." I was breathing heavily now as he pummeled into me, deeper and deeper. I felt like I was going to faint as he took me from behind. And then I felt his right hand slipping in front and rubbing me fast in time with his cock, and I found myself screaming out.

"Oh, shit," he groaned as he pulled out of me.

"What's going on?" I almost started crying as I felt his withdrawal. "Scott ..." I said, my voice as hazy as my eyesight.

"No rubber," he groaned. "Lean forward."

"But ..."

"Shh," he said again and he fell to his knees. "It's my bad." He spread my legs, and I felt his face coming up between my legs.

"Oh my," I squealed as he started licking me. I couldn't believe how intense the feeling was as he licked me. "Oh, Scott!" I screamed as his tongue entered me and finished the job his cock had started. I didn't last very long as his tongue got to work, and I found myself coming within seconds of his tongue sliding in and out of me. I felt myself falling forward after I orgasmed, and he grabbed me up and pulled me into his arms.

"Now to the bedroom," he grunted as he held me next to him. "My turn."

"We could have just gone to the bedroom right away," I mumbled as we walked along the corridor.

"I wanted you to come in there first." He smiled, his eyes glittering down at me. "As a reward."

"Reward for what?"

"For being so brave as to greet me in a bath towel."

"Oh." I blushed.

"But now it's your turn to show me just what you've got."

"Is it now?"

"Yes." He grinned.

"Is it my turn to spank you as well?" I teased him.

"If you want to. If spanking turns you on as much as being spanked."

"It doesn't turn me on," I lied. "Well, it's not the only thing that turns me on. And I didn't even know until today, really."

"That's okay. I didn't know that I would like spanking until today either."

"So why did you do it?"

"I figured they enjoyed it in the movie." He paused. "And I'll admit it, it turned me on in the movie. I figured I would see what it was all about."

"Yeah." I swallowed. "I thought it was pretty kinky in the movie too."

"I knew you had a kinky side."

"I'm not the only one with a kinky side, it seems." I laughed. "If my friend Lacey could hear me now, she'd be cheering."

"Oh? Why's that?" he asked as he picked me up and placed me on his bed.

"Because she thinks that I don't like to admit stuff," I said honestly. "She thinks I keep stuff in, which is true, and because I keep stuff in, I don't get to really try everything I'd like to try."

"You've been pretty straightforward with me," he said.

"I know." I laughed. "You make me brave," I said as I pushed him down onto the bed. "I'm not usually this brave. I'm more talk than anything."

"I'm glad you can let your inner freak out when you're with me."

"Do you think that's strange?" I said as I moved over and sat on top of him. I grabbed his cock with my hands and positioned him between my legs. I looked down at his face, full of desire, and I felt a surge of power as I leaned forward and brushed my breasts against his face.

"Do I think what is strange?" he groaned.

"That I'm so comfortable with you, even though I don't know you well," I moaned as he sucked on my right nipple.

"No," he groaned. "Hold on, let me get a rubber." He reached over to his nightstand and grabbed a condom. "It just means that we're a good fit."

"A good fit?" I giggled as he slid the condom on his hardness. "I guess you could say that."

"I don't mean that my cock fits inside of you perfectly." He winked as his hands grabbed my hips and moved me forward so that I could slide down on top of him. "Though that is also true. Oh, shit." He groaned as I took him inside of me and started rocking my hips back and forth. "I'm not going to last long." He grunted as he reached up and played with my breasts as I rode him.

"That's okay, big boy. We've got all night," I said coyly as I started moving faster and faster, gyrating my hips so that I could feel him deep inside of me.

✦ ✦ ✦

"So I guess we're not going to be doing any work tonight?" I laughed as I played with Scott's chest hair. He was staring at me through sleepy eyes and his hand was rubbing my bare back.

"I don't fancy working in bed." He nodded and yawned. "I guess we can try and get through everything at the office." He smiled. "Tomorrow morning."

"If you think we can." I leaned over and kissed him, still blissful from all our lovemaking.

"We should be able to." He nodded.

"So then why did I have to come over tonight? Admit it, you were just hoping to get me into bed again."

"All right, I admit it." He laughed, his blue eyes sparkling. "I wanted another chance."

"Even though you said I was the one that needed to come to you?" I said, teasing him.

"I knew we liked each other. We just got off on the wrong foot." He said with a smile. "I wasn't going to let that get in our way."

"I was so angry with you for lying to me about having to go out of town. I thought you were blowing me off." I caught myself as I spoke. He didn't know that I knew he'd been lying until I saw him in the office. "So when I saw you in the office and confirmed that what I'd thought was a lie was really a lie, well, I was upset."

"I can understand that." He pursed his lips. "It was a stupid thing to say. I had some stuff come up."

"With your ex?" I asked softly.

"No." His eyes narrowed and his eyes shifted away from me.

"Oh." I bit my lower lip. I could tell he wasn't telling me something and it made me feel uncomfortable. "What happened?"

"It doesn't matter." He looked back at me. "All that matters is the here and now. All that matters in this moment is us."

"I like that." I said with a smile. "I like that a lot."

Chapter Eleven

"Elizabeth?" Lacey faked surprise as she answered the phone. "Fancy hearing from you. I thought you'd skipped the country and were on the run."

"It's been two days, Lacey." I rolled my eyes. Sometimes Lacey acted like my mom.

"Did you run off to Vegas and get married or something?" Lacey said, only half-joking. I'd often said that when I got married it would be an impromptu affair.

"Yeah, I'm married. I'm now Mrs. Scott Taylor. And guess what? Little Scotty Jr. is on the way."

"Ha ha, whatever." Lacey said. "So what's been going on?"

"I've spent the last two nights with Scott," I said happily. "That night when I called you from his bathtub, well, he came home and I did what you said. I went out and seduced him ... well, kinda."

"First off, I never told you to seduce him, and secondly, what is 'kinda' seducing him?"

"So," I said dramatically, "remember that weird movie we watched called *Secretary*?"

"The one where the boss is a pervert and whacks off to his secretary's naked bottom?"

"Yeah, that one." I laughed. "Well, Scott watched it and it kind of turned him on, and he kinda spanked me and I kinda liked it."

"You're *kinda* making me throw up right now," Lacey said, her voice shocked. "Are you kidding me right now? He spanked you and you liked it?"

"Uh huh." I couldn't stop from grinning.

"Like spanked hard or softly?"

"In between."

"You let this man spank you?" Lacey's voice was incredulous. "What?"

"He wasn't trying to hurt me, Lacey. It felt kinky and sexy, and I have to admit, it turned me on."

"Being spanked turns you on now?"

"Yeah, I guess it does." I laughed. "There's nothing wrong with two adults engaging in some harmless fun and foreplay."

"So what are you now? A submissive or something?"

"Lacey, he spanked me, okay? That's it. He didn't whip me or tie me up or tell me to sit still for five hours."

"What would you do if he did?" she asked suspiciously.

"Lacey, are you serious right now? You're the one that told me to go after him if he was what I wanted. You're the one that told me to not let my fear hold me back."

"Yeah, but spanking?"

"Don't knock it till you try it, girlfriend."

"Okay, *girlfriend*." She laughed. "I'll tell my next boyfriend to bend me over and spank me. Harder, sir, harder!"

"You're an idiot." I laughed. "Though you should totally use that in *Play the Player*."

"Of course I'm going to use it in *Play the Player*." She laughed. "So seriously, you spent the last two nights with him?"

"He's really nice, Lacey. I really misjudged him. I really like him. He's not just sexy, but he's funny as well, and he really seems like a genuine guy. Like, he's a manager, right? At this board game company, but he's not in it for the money. He just really loves board games. Like, really loves them. Last night we played this game that he created. It was so much fun. And he was telling me that his siblings don't even know that he created this game, but he told me. How cool is that?"

"That's cool," Lacey said, surprised. "He told you something he hasn't even told his own family?"

"Yeah, he seemed really shy about it. It was totally unexpected and cool. He has all this bravado, and he's such an arrogant, confident guy. It really took me aback."

"You sound like you really like him."

"I really do." I nodded. "I think I judged him way too quickly."

"What are you going to do about Saturday?"

"I'm going to tell him tomorrow." I said. "I don't even care about getting paid. Bob can stuff it. He's not going to fire me. But I don't want Scott to be embarrassed, even if it is just a joke."

"Wow, you really like this guy." Lacey sounded pleased. "I'm happy for you."

"Me too," I said, and then sighed. "I just don't know who this Helen is though."

"Maybe she's his ex-girlfriend."

"Maybe." I sighed. "He blew me off for her and lied about it …" My voice trailed off. "I'm not going to get negative."

"Good," Lacey said. "By the way, I have some news."

"Yeah?"

"I think my dad feels sorry for me, because he just gave me two thousand dollars and told me to buy a flight to come and see you."

"What? No way!"

"Yup, and he told me to give you a grand to help pay rent for two months."

"I can't take that. You're my family."

"Dad said to make you take it." Lacey laughed. "He said he's fed up of hearing us mope around on the phone all day talking about seeing each other. He told me to come down, stay with you for a few months, and see about getting a job."

"What about your book?"

"He told me that most writers have to work if they can't pay the bills and that I'm wasting my life away with him and Mom. He told me to get out there in the real world, have some fun with Eliza, and live a life worth writing about."

"I love your dad," I said, and I honestly did. He was the man I looked to when I wanted a role model of the perfect father. He loved Lacey so much, and I knew it must have hurt him to tell her to move out. She was his little girl, his world, and he would move mountains for her if he could. He was the father I wished I had. He was the man that showed me what I wanted for my kids. When I first met Lacey, I'd been jealous that she'd had someone that loved her so much. I'd spent nights wishing he was my dad too, and my dreams had basically come true. He'd been there for me as if he were my own dad. He'd cared for me like a second daughter. And that had helped to ease some of my own issues regarding my real dad, but it hadn't absolved all my pain.

"Yeah, I love him too. I think I'll keep him," Lacey said and her voice caught as she spoke. I knew she was already starting to feel homesick.

"So when are you coming?" I asked her, wanting to change the subject before she started crying.

"I was thinking in a couple of weeks. Is that okay?"

"That's great." I smiled into the phone. "I can't wait."

"Neither can I," she said softly, but I knew that was only a partial truth.

"So, tomorrow, I think I'm going to tell Scott the truth and hope that he understands and forgives me."

"He'll forgive you. It's not like you went there to trick him on purpose, and you're telling him before you even do the lap dance. So he won't even be embarrassed."

"Yeah, I hope he understands that."

"He will," Lacey said confidently. "I can't wait to meet him next week."

"I can't wait for you to meet him," I agreed. "You're going to love him. And maybe he'll have some really cute friends for you to choose from."

"Choose from?" Lacey giggled. "Like some sort of meat market, and I'm choosing my preferred cut?"

"Ha ha, yeah. You need a good guy."

"Yeah, it would be nice to meet someone. Someone nice, though. And handsome. And rich." She giggled. "Get to work and find me Mr. Right, please."

"Yeah, I'll get on that first thing in the morning." I laughed. "A guy that can help you write *Play the Player*."

"Yeah, I'm sure every guy would be down for that—not!" Lacey said with a laugh. "I mean, they might be down for my new BDSM scene, thanks to you and Scott."

"Lacey," I groaned. "There better not be a chapter about spanking."

"I can't promise anything."

"You're horrible." I laughed. "Just make sure that the character's names aren't Elizabeth and Scott, or I'll sue you."

"Spank me harder, Scott. Just like that weird pervert did in *Secretary*. Oh yes, Scott, just like that. Harder, harder!" Lacey burst out laughing as she mocked me, and I shook my head.

"I guess you want to be the actress now, huh?" I laughed into the phone. "And that's not actually how it went down."

"How did it go down, then?" Lacey asked eagerly.

"I'll never tell." I giggled and then looked at the time. "So get your ticket and let me know about the date and time you arrive, okay?" I said with a yawn. "I think I'm going to have an early night in preparation for my big day tomorrow."

"It'll be fine, Eliza, you'll see."

"I hope so. I sure hope so."

"It'll be fine. And instead of being sealed with a kiss, it will be sealed with a nice smack across your ass."

"Goodnight, Lacey."

"Night, Eliza." She giggled. "Or should I say, Mrs. Spanky?"

And with that, I hung up.

✦ ✦ ✦

My nerves were racing as I walked into the office the next morning. I felt vulnerable and nervous and excited. I wasn't sure how Scott was going to react when I told him I'd been hired to surprise him with a lap dance by someone called H. Smith, who I thought could be the Helen Smith in his phone. I didn't know who she was—probably an upset ex-girlfriend—but I was willing to give him the benefit of the doubt as to why she wanted to get revenge on him like this.

I walked through the corridors of the office building with a small smile on my face. I had a pair of handcuffs in my handbag, and I was going to give them to Scott to tie me up whenever and wherever he wanted. I felt a shiver of excitement run through my body at what I was about to do. Maybe he'd tie me up right away and give me a small spanking, and then bend me over his desk and take me. That would be hot. I took a deep breath as I walked into the office. I was getting ahead of myself now. There was the possibility that he might be a little upset and that probably meant no early morning office sex. Maybe I'd have to wait until this evening.

"Scott, I have something to tell you," I muttered to myself as I walked towards his door. "Scott, look, there's something you should know." I practiced my different lines. "Hey, Scott, you know how I'm an actress and actresses take all sorts of weird jobs?" I said and made a face. I was definitely not going with that line. He might ask what other weird jobs I'd taken before in my life. I was about to walk into the room when I saw Scott talking to some brunette lady wearing extremely high black heels. I stood there and spied for a few seconds to see what was going on.

"Look, Helen, I'm not doing this right now," Scott said, his voice sounding nervous and my heart stopped. Helen? *The* Helen?

"We need to talk, Scott," she said softly, and I saw her placing her hand on his arm. "We can't go on like this." Whoa, what? Go on like this? What was she talking about? My face was flushed as I stood there listening.

"Helen." Scott sounded annoyed.

"What about me, Scott?" Helen moved closer to Scott and my heart started thudding harder.

"I'm not doing this here." Scott looked down at her and said something else that I couldn't hear.

"Who's the new girl? Are you fucking her?" Helen sounded jealous, and I froze as I waited to see what Scott was going to say. This was the moment of truth.

"Of course not. She's my assistant. I wouldn't do that." Scott looked at her like she was crazy, and I stepped back. So he was lying about me.

"You know what I would do if I found out you're fucking your assistant. It would be over," Helen said loudly.

"Helen, please ..." He sighed and shook his hands out. "I don't know what you want me to say. All that matters in this moment is what's going on right now."

I gasped as I heard him saying the words he'd said to me in his bed a couple of nights ago. So it was confirmed. He was a player. He was playing me and this Helen. He was probably sleeping with us both. I felt tears running down my face as I hurried out of the room and down the corridor to the ladies' restroom. I hurried into a stall and cried. I was upset with myself for letting my guard down. I couldn't believe that I had let Scott in and he'd lied to me. He was no better than my dad or Shane. I was going to show him. I was going to give him the sexiest lap dance I could at the office party tomorrow and I was going to embarrass him in front of everyone in the office. That would show him. That would teach him to lie to me.

Chapter Twelve

I must be a good actress. I was able to smile and laugh and flirt with Scott all of Friday night and the day of the office party.

"That's a sexy dress," Scott said as he picked me up and met me at my door.

"Too sexy for an office party?" I asked with a flirtatious smile.

"Never." He grinned. "Maybe too sexy to wear to a dinner with my family, but to an office party, no."

"Dinner with your family?" I asked curiously.

"I want you to come over. Meet Liv and Aiden, Alice, Xander—that's Liv's boyfriend—Chett, and maybe Gabby."

"Oh," I said surprised.

"Unless it's too soon." He made a face at me. "Sorry. I'm not good with this stuff. I don't know if it's too soon."

"No, it's fine," I said with a tight smile. I didn't understand Scott or men. Maybe I would never understand them. Why would he want to introduce me to his family when he was playing me? Had Helen met everyone? Was that why she was so crazy now? Had he made her feel like he loved her and then started treating her like crap?

"Hey, no need to be upset," Scott laughed. "I'm not trying to rush anything here. We can go slow."

"Yeah, I know," I said with a smile as we got into his car.

"Are you excited for the party today?" Scott changed the subject as he started the car.

"Yeah, I'm really excited," I said. "It's going to be really fun."

"I think so too." He grinned. "We can dance and eat and then maybe tonight we can go to a movie."

"Yeah. All of that sounds good," I said as I looked out the window. "Especially the dancing."

"Good. I have to tell you that I'm not the best dancer, but I do give it a try."

"Oh that's fine," I said softly. "I'll be the one leading the way," I said under my breath and smiled to myself. I was going to give him the dance of his life.

✦ ✦ ✦

"Let's sit in this corner," I said and led him to a dark corner in the side of the room.

"You want to sit?" He looked surprised. "I thought you wanted to dance?"

"Yeah, I do," I said and leaned over and whispered in his ear. "I want to give you a private dance."

"A private dance?" His eyes lit up. "What does that mean?"

"It means that I'm wearing a dress and no panties." I winked at him.

"Then dance away." He grinned and I shook my head and laughed. He was so innocent. He had no idea what was about to happen. I smiled to myself, but inside I felt sad. I was sad that he wasn't a genuine person. Even though I knew he was a liar, I still liked him. That made me angry at myself. I still wanted to give him a second chance. Just like I'd done for my dad. I'd always made excuses for him. Every time he'd said he was going to show up and take me to dinner, I'd said okay. I'd really thought, *This time it's going to happen. This time he seems genuine. He wants to see me. I'm his daughter. Why would he lie to me? He loves me, right?* And then I'd sit in the living room waiting all day, staring out of the window, waiting for him to show up, waiting until it was dark outside and I had to go to bed. And he never came. And each time that happened, I lost a small piece of my heart and soul to disappointment and heartache. I didn't understand how some people could lie so easily, and carelessly, without even given a thought to the other person. My dad hadn't cared that he'd let me down. And now—now Scott didn't care that he was playing me. Drawing me close to him, telling me about his family, inviting me to dinner, acting as if he liked me and could see a real future for us. How could he play with my feelings like that when he knew that he still had something going on with Helen?

I turned to him then, looked at his handsome face, his expectant boyish grin, his big blue eager eyes, and a part of me broke. I leaned forward and kissed him hard. I kissed him for every part of me that really liked every part of him, and then I stepped back. I couldn't allow myself to think about what I liked about him or fall into the trap of his soul. I pushed him down on the chair and started moving in time to the music.

"This is so hot." He laughed as his hands slid up under my dress to touch my ass.

"No touching," I said and kissed the side of his cheek. I reached down and grabbed my handbag and pulled out the handcuffs I had in there and quickly tied his arms to the chair.

"Handcuffs huh?" He raised an eyebrow and shifted in the chair. "I knew you were kinky."

"Yup," I said and shifted on his lap, so that his hardness was right between my legs. I moved back and forth on his lap and he groaned as he sat there. His eyes turned dark with desire and he grunted.

"This is so hot, but I'm scared someone is going to see us." He laughed and looked out at the party.

"Do you care?" I said, and I kissed him before he could answer. I jumped up, turned around, and sat back down on his lap, rubbing my ass against his crotch and grinding until I thought he was as hard as could be. I was turning both of us on at the same time, and I was having a hard time staying focused.

I reached down and massaged his hardness through his pants before pulling it out.

"Elizabeth?" Scott said with wild eyes. "What are you doing?"

"Shh," I said and leaned forward to kiss him again, before sliding down on him. "Oooh," I moaned against his lips as I moved back and forth on his lap, completely entrancing us both with my special dance. I bounced around on his lap and took him deep inside of me, crying out every time I slammed down on him. He came hard and fast and we kissed passionately as I orgasmed on top of him.

"What the fuck?" I heard someone shout as reality started to set in. I paused and looked behind me and saw that about twenty people were standing at the other side of the room and staring at us, Helen being front and center. This was it, then. I swallowed hard as I stood up and pulled my dress down. I looked at Scott and his face was red as he looked at the crowd.

"Oh, shit," he said.

"I guess your girlfriend is going to dump you now, liar," I hissed at him.

"Girlfriend?" Scott looked at me in confusion. "Elizabeth," he said huskily, "zip me up and take these handcuffs off my wrists."

"Why? Don't you want everyone to see the hard cock you just fucked me with?" I glared down at him.

"What are you talking about?" Scott's voice grew louder. "Undo these handcuffs. There are people in the room staring at us."

"Sure," I said after a few seconds and undid the handcuffs slowly. The room was quiet and I knew that everyone was still staring at us in shock. I'd done my job perfectly. Maybe even more perfectly than Helen Smith expected. I'd well and truly embarrassed Scott now. Not only had I given him a lap dance, but we'd had sex as well. There was no way he'd live that down.

"Elizabeth, what is going on?" Scott said as he quickly zipped himself up. "Did you forget where we were?"

"You forgot as well," I said with a smirk. "You weren't complaining when I slipped your cock out and started riding it."

"Well, I was caught up in the moment," he said with a small smile, and then his face changed as he looked past my shoulder and saw Helen walking up towards us. "Fuck," he said under his breath, and I looked away from his face. It hurt too much to know that this man I had really and truly liked had lied to me.

"Scott, I'm going to need to see you in my office. This goes against our office protocol," Helen said in a snooty voice, and my heart stopped for a few seconds. What was she talking about? Those weren't the words I'd expected to hear from her mouth. I'd expected to see her crying and telling him that he had destroyed her with his cheating.

"It was some innocent office party fun," Scott said with a sigh. "Let it go, Helen."

"You're read the HR manual, Scott. You know that fornicating in the office is against company rules."

Company rules?

"Get over it." Scott's voice was annoyed again. "I'm fed up of you trying to make my life miserable just because I'm not interested in you." My gaze flew to him as he spoke. *Oh, shit*, I thought as a sinking feeling hit me. I'd messed up.

"What's going on, Scott?" I swallowed hard. "Who's this Helen?" I pointed at her. Please God, tell me that Helen is his current or ex-girlfriend. Please make Scott the bastard I thought he was.

"Fuck it, I didn't want to get you involved in this. I didn't think it was fair as you were new to the company," Scott sighed. "But I suppose I have to tell you now. Helen here is the HR manager, and she's had it in for me since I blew her off at last year's office party."

"You didn't blow me off," Helen said, looking angry.

"You asked me to fuck you and I said no," Scott said, his tone deathly. "I consider that me blowing you off." He sighed and then looked at me. "For the last year, Helen has been calling me and texting me non-stop, saying she wants to do all sorts of things to me. At first it was sexual, and then she started getting angry, saying she was going to bring me down. She's practically been stalking me. I've been trying to deal with it my way, but she seems to want to see me fired. That weekend we met, I lied because she kept blowing up my phone and when I called her to find out what her problem was, she said to me that if I could pick up a girl at the bar and fuck her, I could fuck her too. That's when I knew she was stalking me and that I needed to speak to the president of the company about what was going on. I didn't want to involve you or scare you, so I was going to deal with her and then call you."

"But in the office yesterday, you told her you didn't like me like that. I thought you guys were ..." My voice trailed off.

"I didn't want her to know." Scott sighed. "What we have is special. And I like my job and I like you working for me. I didn't want either of us to get in trouble or fired." He paused then and frowned. "I didn't know you saw us talking in the office yesterday."

"Oh. I didn't want to interrupt." My face went red. "I need to tell you something, Scott." I said, my voice cracking.

Helen, who had been silent until that point, looked at me then and gave me a sweet serene smile. "You can leave now, Elizabeth. Good job tonight. Tell Bob that I will be sending in a thousand-dollar bonus for you. I'm pleased with how you really put yourself into the role."

"Wait, what?" Scott's eyes narrowed and my heart thudded. "What role? What's Helen talking about, Elizabeth?"

"Oh, didn't you know?" Helen smiled sweetly, though her eyes looked vindictive. "Elizabeth is an actress who works for Candy Grams, a company where you can hire people to do whatever you want them to do. She was hired by me two weeks ago for this position to fool you into thinking she liked you, just so she could embarrass you at this party. Everything she has been saying and doing is an act."

"Elizabeth?" He looked at me, his eyes shocked. "Is this true?"

"Yeah, she even asked for more money." Helen said and laughed before I could speak. "She negotiated for more money after she saw your photo."

"You got this assignment two weeks ago?" He frowned. "Before we met at the bar?"

"I can explain," I said weakly.

"And you'd seen my photo already?" He frowned. "So at the bar, you knew who I was?"

"Kinda ... I—I didn't know if ..." My voice trailed off. I didn't know what to say. I'd well and truly fucked myself.

"So it was all an act." He jumped up. "Your rage, your hurt, your story about your dad. All of it was an act."

"No, of course not." I jumped up and grabbed his arm. "Please, Scott. Let's talk about this."

"You truly fucked me in every way possible." His head fell back and he laughed bitterly. "And *you* tried to make me feel bad."

"It's not like that. I slept with you because I like you. And I was going to tell you the truth. I really was."

"You're no better than a prostitute," he said, looking disgusted.

"I'd say an escort." Helen said as she looked at me with a superior look. "She's basically an escort."

"I'm not a prostitute or an escort. I slept with you because I liked you. I like you, Scott."

"So why didn't you tell me what was going on, if you like me?"

"Because I saw you and Helen in the office, and I got confused. I thought she was your girlfriend and you were cheating on her with me and lying to us both."

"So essentially you were lying to me, yet you didn't trust me?" He looked at me with narrowed eyes and a tight voice.

I nodded and took a deep breath. My chest felt tight and I could feel that tears were about to fall. "You have to understand, Scott. I wanted to trust you. I just had a hard time. I came to your office to tell you and I saw you talking with her. I saw you telling her that all that matters in that moment was what was going on then, just like you told me."

"What?" He frowned.

"You said that same sentence to me and her. 'All that matters in this moment is what's going on right now,'" I cried out. "I thought it was your thing, what you say to all your girls."

"It's a bloody saying, Elizabeth." He looked angry. "It was obviously applicable in both situations. Don't worry about what's going on in my life if everything is functioning fine for us. When I said that to you, I meant you were the only girl for me, there were no exes of importance, and when I said it to Helen, I meant that I'm doing my job quite well, so she should just focus on that."

"I didn't know that," I said. "If I'd known, I would have come to you still. Please, Scott, I messed up. Can we at least talk about this?"

"Save it." He shook his head. "I'm done. I can't deal with this. I can't believe you would do this to me. All you've done is judge me and not trust me. And you're the one that's been lying this entire time."

"Scott," I reached out to touch his arm and he shook me off.

"Don't," he said. He stared at me for a few seconds and his eyes looked pained as he gazed at me. "I thought we had something special. I thought that from the very first time I met you. I knew there was a fragility to you. I knew you'd experienced hurt. But you still had spunk. You were shy and naïve at the same time as being bold and kinky. I never knew what to expect. I loved that. I thought, here's a girl that will constantly surprise me. I thought, here's someone that could be really special in my life. Shit, I thought you could be the one. But you fooled me. You got me. I guess you really are a good actress. Look out

Hollywood, here comes Elizabeth Jeffries! I'll look for you at the Oscars next year. I'm sure you'll pick up the award for Best Actress."

"Scott." I bit my lower lip. "Please let me explain."

"There's nothing you have to say that I want to hear." He shook his head. "I'm done. I don't need more drama in my life. I have more important things to deal with right now. Like keeping my job."

"I'm sorry," I said and grabbed my bag. I walked out of the room slowly, feeling embarrassed and heartbroken. How had it all gone so wrong so quickly? How had I fucked it up again? I walked back to my car and let my tears flow. It was over and I'd ruined everything. And all for what? Two hundred dollars?

Part II

The Second Time I Worked For a Taylor Brother

A Month Later

Chapter Thirteen

"Bob called. He said he wants you to call him as soon as possible." Lacey looked up at me as I walked into the living room. "How was your shower?"

"Hot." I smiled at her and then groaned. "Ugh, I don't want to talk to Bob."

"Sorry for answering your phone. He kept calling, so I thought it was something important."

"Oh, I don't care about that," I said. "I just don't want to talk to him." I looked at the coffee table in front of Lacey strewn with papers, and I smiled. "First draft nearly done?"

"Are you joking?" Lacey screeched. "I'm so lost. I don't know if I have too much sex or too little sex."

"Why don't you read some to me, and I can let you know?"

"Really?" Lacey said. "I just printed out this scene, and I don't know if it's too much."

"Go ahead." I settled into the couch next to her. "I'm not doing anything today."

"You don't want to call Bob back first?"

"I don't want to dress up like a clown this weekend." I shook my head and crossed my legs on the cushions. "And thanks to your dad giving you rent money for two months, I don't need to."

"Yeah." Lacey nodded. "You needed a break," she said and looked at me for a few seconds. I knew she was debating internally as to whether to ask me how I was doing. We had only spoken about what had happened with Scott once and I'd never mentioned it again. She knew that I was the sort of person that brought something up when I wanted to talk about it. She knew that after what had happened with Shane, I was very careful to not talk too much, because I didn't want to make myself sadder.

"Go ahead," I said and nodded at her encouragingly. "I'm waiting."

"Okay." She smiled nervously and cleared her throat. She leaned forward and picked up some of the papers on the coffee table and shuffled them into some sort of order. "Midnight is the witching hour. Midnight is the hour that Cinderella fled from her prince. It's the hour that the prince turned into a werewolf and it's the hour that I experienced my first blissful night. I can still feel the touch of his hand on the curve of my butt, as if it were an extension of my body. I can still feel the tingles, smell the fear and excitement, hear the loud decisive sound of his hand against my raw skin. Slap. Slap. Slap. Bliss. Five fingers and one palm. Who knew that they could cause such bliss?" Lacey paused and looked at my face and her hand flew to her mouth as she stared at my slightly awestruck expression. "Oh my God, Elizabeth, I'm so sorry. I wasn't thinking."

"It's fine," I said, not even blinking as I sat there in shock and sadness.

"I didn't mean to read you this scene. I forgot."

"It's okay." I reached out and touched her hand. "Don't feel bad. It's not as if Scott and I were the only people that have ever engaged in spanking. Many bedrooms across the county have couples experiencing that bliss, as you put it."

"I feel so insensitive," she said and sighed, her brown eyes looking sad. "Sorry."

"Lacey, it's fine. Really and truly," I said and jumped up. "Though I'm going to go and get some wine. I need a drink. Want a glass?"

"Yes, please." She nodded.

"Okay, hold on," I said and hurried to the kitchen and grabbed two glasses and a bottle of Moscato that I had chilling in the fridge. I grabbed a box of cookies as well and headed back to the living room. "You know, it's really quite funny," I said as I set the glasses down on the coffee table.

"What's funny?" Lacey asked, a confused expression on her face as she looked up from the page she was working on. Her lips were black with ink stains and her long brown hair hung in loose waves around her face. She was wearing an old Mickey Mouse t-shirt and a pair of black sweatpants, and I felt a surge of warmth in my stomach as I stared at her. I was so glad that Lacey was here with me.

"The fact that your book *Play the Player* has a spanking scene after how outraged you were when I told you that Scott and I had engaged in spanking as foreplay."

"I was a little shocked and just teasing at first." She grinned. "But then I thought about it, and spanking is all the rage these days. *Play the Player* needs some spanking. That's what makes it so hot and sexy."

"Is that what makes all the romance books hot these days?" I said and laughed. "Hot and sexy?"

"The sexier the better." She grinned. "I want my book to be so hot and sexy that people are blushing just opening the book."

"Um, okay." I giggled. "You need to write about a bit more than spanking then."

"Yeah." She laughed. "I guess I do." She paused and then looked at me for a few seconds before speaking again. "So, have you spoken to Scott?"

"Who?" I said and then shook my head. "Nope."

"Have you tried contacting him?"

"Nope." I rested my head against the back of the couch. "He hasn't contacted me either. He hates me."

"I'm sure he doesn't hate you, Eliza."

"Yeah, I'm sure he does and if he doesn't hate me, he dislikes me very much and thinks I'm a crazy bitch and a liar."

"I'm sure if you explained to him what happened, he would understand."

"Lacey, I explained to him what happened. He didn't care. He thought I was a hypocrite for being all hard on him when I was lying in the first place."

"You can at least ..." Her voice trailed off as she saw the look on my face. "Fine, don't contact him."

"There's just no point," I said.

"Yeah." She nodded and grabbed the bottle of wine and filled up the glasses. "Here you go," she said as she handed me a glass. "You should call Bob, see what job he has for you. It might help to get out of the house."

"Instead of sitting here and bothering you, you mean?" I laughed.

"You're not bothering me!" she exclaimed. "This is your house, Eliza."

"Girl, you know this is your home as well, and you're right, I might as well see what job Bob has for me. Maybe it will pay for a nice spa trip."

"Spa trip?" Lacey raised an eyebrow.

"A day trip at least." I giggled. "I really want a mud bath and a massage."

"Yeah, that would be cool," she said and stretched. "A deep tissue massage from some guy called Brody with big muscles and strong hands." She moaned and closed her eyes. "And he'll knead all my stress away. Oh, I can feel it now. And I'll be naked and he'll massage every part of my body. In an appropriate way, of course. And then he'll scrub me down with Dead Sea salt and exfoliate my skin and then he'll turn me over and—"

"Um, Lacey, is this a scene for your book or for your real sex life?" I asked her, grinning.

"What?" she said as she opened her eyes, her face slightly flushed.

"Lacey, you're not going to a day spa to have an orgasm. You need to find a boyfriend."

"I know," she groaned. "Writing this book is getting me all hot and bothered, and what do I have? Nothing!"

"You have Magnus."

"Magnus?" She frowned. "Who the fuck is Magnus?"

"That dildo I gave you in college?"

"That ten-inch dildo you gave me?" She burst out laughing. "You did not seriously think that I was going to be using that thing. Magnus is in my closet at home."

"Sad, poor Magnus."

"Poor me, you mean." She laughed and I joined her. "We need to go out and try to meet some guys."

"Yeah," I said. "I guess so."

"When you're ready, anyway," she said.

"I can still be your wing woman," I said and grinned. "Hold on, let me go and call Bob and I'll be right back. Maybe we can go out this weekend."

"Yeah, that would be cool." She grinned up at me eagerly. "We can go dancing … or maybe not dancing," she said sheepishly, and I rolled my eyes as I walked out of the room. Lacey was going to want to go dancing, no matter what she said. That was one of our go-to girls nights out. We both loved to shake our asses to Top 40 pop and hip hop, and there was nothing like getting drunk and flirting with random guys. It was probably long overdue that we should go out and party and have some fun.

I called Bob's number and waited for him to pick up the phone. Our last conversation hadn't been pleasant. I'd shouted at him, and he'd told me that I was unprofessional and that I was fired. Of course, he hadn't meant it. He'd been calling me every day for the last month begging me to come back to work for him. He needed me more than I needed him. I was the only one that was willing to put up with his bullshit pay and shady jobs.

"Elizabeth," he said, his voice exuberant as he answered the phone. "So good to hear from you," he said, sounding like a happy uncle hearing from his favorite niece.

"Hi, Bob," I said, already losing patience with him. "I'm just returning your call. What's up?"

"I had a request for you."

"A request for me?" I said, my heart beating fast as I grew hopeful.

"Well, not you in particular." His tone changed. "Just a pretty young woman."

"And I'm the only one that fit the bill, huh?"

"It pays a grand a week."

"A grand a week?" I said, my eyes widening. "And what do I have to do for the grand? Fuck him every night?"

"Elizabeth!" he said, sounding shocked. "You know I would never ask you to do a job like that."

"Uh huh," I said and rolled my eyes. "What's the job?"

"There's this guy. He wants to hire you to pretend to be his girlfriend."

"Uh huh," I said and started laughing. "Bob, you just told me you wouldn't hire me to do a job like this."

"It's not what you think. He wants to make a girl jealous. That's his purpose. He's in love with someone else. He wants her to think she has some competition."

"Excuse my language, but what the fuck?" I was annoyed. "That's ridiculous. He likes someone, yet he's hiring a fake girlfriend?"

"I guess he wants to make sure that this girl is the one," Bob said. "Look, I don't bloody know what's going on, but I met the guy and he seems legit. And he seems to really love this girl."

"He loves this girl and instead of telling her, he's hiring a fake girlfriend?"

"I can't tell you why people do what they do," Bob said. "But this guy is a lawyer, and I think he's legit."

"Uh huh." I frowned. "Anything else you wanted to ask me, Bob? Because I'm about to hang up on you, and I'm telling you that I'm not taking this job."

"So you're telling me I have to tell Aiden Taylor no, then?" Bob said and I froze.

"What's this guy's name?" I said in disbelief.

"His name is Aiden Taylor."

"Oh, hell no," I said. "What's the girl's name that he likes? Wait, don't tell me, is it Liv? No, wait, that's his sister. Is it Alice?"

"Yeah, how did you know?" Bob sounded surprised.

"Bloody hell. Can't this family leave me alone?" I said, my face burning as I realized that my new client was Scott's brother.

"You know him?"

"No. Yes. Ugh, not really." I sighed.

"So you're going to take the job?"

"No," I said adamantly, but then something in me started to get excited. Maybe this was a way to see Scott again. Maybe if I could just see him, I could explain. "Maybe. I want to meet this Aiden first."

"I can set a meeting up tomorrow if you want."

"Yeah. I guess that's fine. Do not tell him I've taken the job. Just tell him that I'm willing to meet him to see if I can help him."

"Okay." Bob sounded gleeful. I knew he was already picturing his new pickup truck or whatever he was going to buy with the money he made. "Come to the office tomorrow at 11 a.m. and I'll have you guys meet."

"Okay." I hung up and buried my face in my hands. I had no idea if I was making a mistake, but I knew that this was fate's way of giving me a second chance. At least I hoped it was.

✦ ✦ ✦

"Hi, I'm Aiden." A tall man stood up and reached his hand out to me. He had a huge smile on his face and his big blue eyes reminded me of Scott, only Aiden had darker hair.

"Elizabeth," I said and shook his hand. I stared into his eyes to see if my name rang any bells.

"Nice to meet you," he said with a small smile. "Shall we have a seat?"

"Sure," I said and sat down in the chair next to his. "Where's Bob?"

"He said he was going to Burger King," Aiden said, and I could feel his eyes on my face. "He had some coupon that was going to expire today or something."

"Of course." I laughed and sat back, pushing my breasts out. I concentrated on Aiden's face to see if he was going to look at my boobs, but he continued staring at my face. I liked that. I was testing him to see if he really liked this Alice girl, or if he still had eyes for other women. "So tell me why we're here, Aiden. I don't really understand."

"Sure." He nodded and he grabbed his phone. "Hold on, I want to show you something."

"Okay," I said and watched him scroll through his phone.

"See this?" He handed me the phone and I looked down at the screen. It was a photo of a pretty girl with big blue eyes, blonde hair and a goofy smile.

"Yeah."

"This is the love of my life," he said, his voice light. "Her name is Alice. I feel like I've known her all my life and I basically have. She's my sister's best friend. I've loved her forever and I want to spend my life with her."

"Okay, wow," I said and gazed at him. "Why are we here again?"

"See this?" He grinned and scrolled to another photo and showed it to me. The other photo was of another pretty girl. This one had brown hair and brown eyes. I felt my heart pounding as I looked at the photo. Please don't let him say that this was the other love of his life.

"Yeah?"

"This is my sister, Liv."

"Oh, that's Liv," I said and stared at the photo some more. This was Scott's sister, the one that he'd wanted me to meet.

"Yeah." Aiden frowned as he looked at me. "You know her?"

"No, no, sorry, continue."

"Oh, okay." He looked at me carefully for a few seconds and then continued. "Liv and Alice are the most fun, beautiful, wonderful women, but they're both very immature. They play a lot of games, have a lot of fun, and sometimes I don't know what's serious to them and what isn't." He sighed. "I love my sister and I love Alice. I really want to pursue Alice, but I need to see if she's ready for a real relationship. And to see if she really cares for me or not." He made a face. "I know this must seem lame, but I thought that by hiring you to be my pretend girlfriend/mystery girl in my life, I could kind of force Alice's hand and see where we really stand."

"That's a bit risky, isn't it?" I said with a frown.

"Yes." He nodded. "But it's a calculated risk that I'm ready to take."

"Calculated risk, huh?" I laughed. "Spoken like a true lawyer."

"Well, you know."

"What does your family think about it?"

"Liv doesn't know." He laughed. "I've spoken to my brothers Chett and Scott, and they both think it could be a good idea."

"Oh, really?" I leaned forward. I wanted to ask him about Scott. Where he was? What he was doing? How was he? Had he ever talked about me?

"Yeah, but it's really my decision," he said seriously. "I wouldn't expect anything untoward from you. Just have you show up at a few events to see how Alice reacts, plus maybe you can leave some posts on my Facebook account and stuff like that."

"That seems innocent enough," I said thoughtfully.

"Yes, nothing crazy," he said. "I'm willing to pay three grand a week."

"Three grand a week?" I said and frowned. That bastard Bob was only paying me a grand. I was going to really confront him about how much money he was taking.

"Is that not enough?" Aiden looked worried.

"No, that's great." I said and leaned back for a few moments. "Are you sure this is something you want to go through with, Aiden? Sometimes games and these small lies aren't the way to go."

"I'm sure," he said, his eyes determined and bright as he looked at me. I was slightly taken aback by how much he resembled Scott and it made my heart ache.

"Okay, then. I'm in," I said and leaned forward and shook his hand. "Just let me know what you want me to do and it's done."

"Great. Thank you. You don't know how much this means to me." He jumped up and pulled me towards him and gave me a quick hug. "Thank you, Elizabeth."

"Thank me if everything works out with Alice."

"Yeah." He nodded and stepped back. "Let's hope so."

"If she's the right one for you, it will work out," I said with a soft smile. "Everything works out if it's meant to be."

"Yeah, I believe that as well," he said, and then he looked into my eyes, and I felt as if he were trying to glimpse into my soul. "We'll have to grab lunch this week to chat and figure out how this is going to work, and I hope to get to know you as well, Elizabeth." He smiled. "Seeing as we're going to be spending a lot of time together."

"Oh, there's not much to know," I said with a small smile.

"There's always a lot to know." He gave me a knowing look. "I'll get it out of you."

I laughed and didn't say anything else. Little did he know that I had a past with his brother.

"I'll let you go now, but maybe we can meet up tomorrow for lunch and talk?"

"Yeah, that sounds good," I said. "Meet you here?"

"Yeah, we can meet here." He nodded. "See you later, Elizabeth."

"Bye, Aiden," I said and watched as he left the room. I was about to call Lacey and tell her what had just happened, when I decided to call my mom instead. I hadn't spoken to her in a couple of weeks, and I knew she was likely waiting for me to call. I'd call her while I was still in a good mood and hopefully she wouldn't bring me down.

✦ ✦ ✦

"Hello?" My mom answered the phone in a soft questioning tone, though I knew she had caller ID on her phone.

"Hey, Mom, it's me."

"Elizabeth?"

"I'm the only one that calls you Mom," I said in an exasperated tone.

"I was just checking," she said defensively.

"How are you, Mom?" I asked, not wanting to get into it already.

"Okay." She sighed, a long deep sigh that told me that she wasn't really okay.

"What's wrong, Mom?"

"They cut my food stamp allowance," she said in a small voice. "I'm hungry."

"You don't have food?" I said in a small voice.

"Nothing good," she said in a bitter tone.

"Do you want me to send you some money?"

"No, I've got my Social Security money and food stamps," she said in a pitiful voice.

"Mom, I can send you some money if you're hungry."

"I didn't think you cared," she said. "I haven't heard from you in months."

"Mom, I called you three weeks ago." I sighed, regretting that I'd even called this time around.

"I thought that I was hurt when your dad left, but nothing hurts more than when you own child, that you pushed out with no painkillers, barely calls you."

"Mom." I sighed. "I'll send you some money, okay?"

"Don't send it Western Union. They steal the money. Put it in my bank account. I have an account with Chase now."

"They let you reopen it?" I said, surprised.

"I went to a new branch. They didn't check the system." She sounded almost gleeful. "That's not my problem."

"What if they take the money I deposit and use it to pay off your other account?"

"They can't do that. That's my money!" she screeched. "That would be stealing."

"Yeah," I said, though I was thinking that it's not stealing if you owe them money for insufficient funds in another account.

"Can you send the money today?" she asked hopefully.

"Why?" I asked suspiciously.

"So I can go to the store," she said. "To get some food."

"Uh huh." I said, but I didn't say anything else. I knew she wasn't going to get food. I knew she wasn't hungry. I knew what she really wanted.

"Don't uh huh me, young lady."

"Sorry, Mom," I said and stared at the wall. "So how are you, asides from being hungry?"

"Fine." She sighed. "I'm still getting headaches, but the bloody doctor won't prescribe me any oxycontin. He doesn't care about my pain."

"I see." I bit my lower lip. My mom had had a prescription drug problem for years, though she would never admit that she was an addict.

"It's ridiculous. If he prescribed it, I could get it cheaper from the state." She complained. "You should be upset too."

"Yeah," I said, not saying anything else. I knew that's what she wanted my cash for. I knew she wanted drugs so she could self-medicate. I knew she was an addict. I knew she had problems. And I'd tried for years to talk to her, but she had never listened. And her addiction wasn't bad enough to warrant the state demanding she go to rehab. I didn't even bring it up anymore because it only made her angry at me. I couldn't deal with the anger and stress anymore.

"How's Lacey?" she asked, her voice soft. My mom loved Lacey, almost more than she loved me. I wasn't sure why, but I figured it was because Lacey had never-ending patience and always listened to my mom as if she were the most important person in the world.

"Good. She's staying with me right now. She's writing a book."

"Good for her. Good for both you girls," my mom said, her voice chipper, and my heart broke at how easy it was for her to go from surly to happy. I loved my happy mom. I hated my surly addict mom. "You're really going for your dreams. Not going to make a mistake like me. Marry some bum who'll leave you and your little girl and not look back."

"Yeah, well, I'm no closer to getting married and neither is Lacey," I said with a small sigh. "But, Mom, I have to go, okay? I have to go and do something for work. Email me your bank account information, and I'll deposit some money tomorrow."

"Okay, honey. I love you," she said, and I hung up quickly. I walked out of Candy Grams, my heart heavy, and sighed. No wonder I was so fucked up in the head. I quickly called Lacey to try and turn my mood around.

"Hey, Eliza, what's going on?" she asked excitedly. "Was it Scott's brother? Was Scott there?"

"Yes, it was Scott's brother, and no, he wasn't there," I said softly.

"What happened? What's wrong?" she asked, her voice concerned. "What did that jackass do?"

"Nothing." I sighed. "I just spoke to my mom."

"Oh." Lacey said and we were both silent. "How is she?"

"She needs to borrow some money, for food," I said lightly.

"Oh," Lacey said, and I knew she knew that food was the last thing my mom wanted to buy. "Want to do something this afternoon? Go somewhere fun?"

"Don't you have to work?"

"Let's bunk off," she said. "We both deserve a break. Maybe we can go and catch a movie down by the lake. Maybe an old black-and-white movie."

"Are you sure? You hate black-and-white movies."

"I'm sure." She giggled. "I just need popcorn."

"Okay, that sounds good. Thank you," I said softly, and I could feel tears welling up in my eyes. Lacey was truly the best friend that anyone could ask for. I'd been cursed with two horrible parents, but Lacey made up for them in more ways that anyone could ever imagine.

"No, thank you," she said. "I've just been sitting here trying to figure out a way to write 'he had a hard cock' in the most sensual way, without it sounding like porn."

"Oh, what were your options?" I said with a laugh.

"Hard cock, gigantic penis, bulging manhood, sensual stick, growing erection, throbbing member, strawberry lollipop."

"Strawberry lollipop?" I said and burst out laughing.

"Yes, strawberry lollipop." She giggled. "I have chocolate lollipop as well."

"Oh, Lacey." I groaned. "What did you decide upon?"

"Hard cock." She laughed. "Might as well keep it simple, right?"

"Yeah, you don't want to confuse your readers. They might wonder what's going on if they start reading about the main character eating a chocolate lollipop."

"Or being fucked by a chocolate lollipop," she said with a giggle.

"Yeah, you might find some reader contacting you asking you to let her know where she can find a chocolate lollipop to fuck her."

"Eww, you're gross."

"No, I'm not." I laughed. "I'm just telling you what to expect, Dr. Ruth."

"I'm not giving sex advice," Lacey said. "I don't think anyone will be contacting me for advice based on a book called *Play the Player*."

"You'd be surprised." I giggled. "Okay, I'm on my way home and then we can go to the movie."

"Sounds good," she said. "See you soon."

"Yeah, see you in a bit," I said and hung up the phone. I looked up at the sky and just stood there for a few minutes, wondering what the next day was going to bring.

Chapter Fourteen

"Hey, Elizabeth," Aiden said as I picked up the phone. "How's it going?"

"Alice liked a post on my page today," I laughed. "So we definitely know that she knows about me."

"Oh, Alice." He laughed. "Did she leave a comment?"

"No," I said. "So what's next? We've been fake-dating online for two weeks now. What's your plan?"

"I'm going to call her and let it slip that we're going on a date."

"To where?"

"To where what?" He sounded confused.

"Where are we going on the date?" I said with a small smile. "I know we're not really going, but if Alice asks you where we're going, she's going to expect an answer and you're going to need to have something on the tip of your tongue."

"Oh, I guess," he said. "Dinner and a movie?"

"No," I said. "That sounds too intimate. You want to make her slightly jealous, not have her thinking she doesn't have a shot."

"Then what?"

"Maybe an art exhibit?" I suggested. "It's casual, but still a fun date."

"Yeah, I guess. Um, should I say we're going to the Museum of Sex? Get her mind rolling in the gutter?"

"Aiden!" I almost shouted. "You're a typical man. No, don't say we're going to the Museum of Sex. Say you're taking me to an exhibit, Picasso or Monet or whoever. See what exhibits the museums have right now."

"Yeah, I'll do that. I think that there might be a Degas exhibit in town right now."

"Okay, that's our date, then. If she asks, we're going to a Degas exhibit."

"Okay, then." He laughed. "Oh, and by the way, do you play flag football?"

"Nope," I said, and he laughed.

"Honest answer, but I need you to start playing."

"Oh, why?"

"We're all going to be playing in this league, and I want you to come."

"Who is 'all'?"

"Alice, Liv, my brothers, Liv's fiancé, Xander, and his brother Henry."

"Your brothers Scott and Chett?" I asked softly, my heart thudding. Oh my God, was I finally going to see Scott again? I wondered what he would do if he saw me. What would he think? Did he still hate me?

"Yeah. Good memory," he said sounding surprised. "I only mentioned them once before."

"Yeah, I'm an actress, remember?" I said quickly. "I've got a good memory."

"Yeah." He laughed. "Okay, so we have a match this week. I'll text you the info and you can come, okay?"

"Okay, sounds good." I took a deep breath. "So I'm going to meet Alice as well?"

"Yeah." His voice softened. "She'll be there as well."

"You should just ask her out, Aiden."

"I will," he said with a sigh. "I just need to make sure that this is something she really wants as well. Because this is for forever for me. And if she's not ready for forever, I'll be heartbroken."

"I understand," I said softly. "I'll talk to you later, Aiden," I said and hung up. I lay back on my bed and closed my eyes. What would it feel like to be loved by someone that much? This Alice didn't even know how lucky she was. Aiden absolutely adored her. I only hoped that she was worthy of his love. I was scared that I was going to meet her and think she wasn't good enough for Aiden. Or that she didn't love him like he loved her. I was praying that she was the one for him. I wasn't sure I could handle being a part of another heartbreak, even if it wasn't my own.

✦ ✦ ✦

"Lacey, I cannot believe I have to play flag football." I groaned into the phone as I walked to the field where I was meeting Aiden.

"Girl, who cares about the football? I'm more concerned about the fact that you're going to see Scott again!"

"Yeah, there's that as well," I said casually, though my heart was racing.

"How are you feeling?"

"Nervous as hell," I said, my throat dry.

"Understandable," Lacey said. "I'm sure it will be fine. I bet he'll see you and beg you to take him back."

"I sincerely doubt that," I said. "Especially when he hears I'm there with Aiden."

"You're not going to allow him to think that, are you?"

"Hell no." I laughed. "I'm going to tell him as soon as I get an opportunity."

"Good," Lacey said. "I wish I could have come."

"Yeah, me too. Maybe you can come to the next game. Hopefully it will be fun. I can't believe I'm going to be meeting Scott's whole family."

"I know, it's crazy."

"I hope he's not still angry at me," I said, as my stomach curdled. "That would suck."

"Girl, just be prepared for a cold reception from him and then go from there."

"Yeah." I sighed. "I know. Eek, I'm seeing them on the field. I'll call you when I'm on my way back, okay?"

"Okay. Good luck," Lacey said and hung up. I put my phone back into my bag and ran onto the field, taking several deep breaths as I approached the group. I ran over to Aiden, and I could see Alice staring at me with big eyes.

"There you are, darling." I ran over to Aiden and gave him a huge smile.

"Lizzie!" he exclaimed and started beaming at me. I thought he was putting it on a bit strong, but who was I to say anything? I could feel Alice staring at me with a stiff face, and I hid a small smile. So maybe this girl did like him after all.

"Sorry I'm late." I wrinkled my nose as I gave Aiden a sorry voice.

"You're not late," he said and grabbed me. I stumbled into his arms and stood there awkwardly as he gave me a quick hug and kiss on the cheek. "You're right on time." He grinned at me, his blue eyes sparkling. I looked over at Alice and I saw a dart of unhappiness crossing her face. I felt bad about the way she was feeling, but at least she was exhibiting signs of caring about Aiden. "Elizabeth, I want you to meet Alice. Alice is my sister Liv's best friend." He nodded at Alice, and I saw them exchange a quick look. "And Alice, I want you to meet Elizabeth, a good friend of mine." I almost laughed at that. Good friend, indeed. I thought it was cute that though Aiden was playing this game, he didn't want her to think I was his girlfriend.

"Hi," Alice said and she smiled at me, a light in her blue eyes that showed me she was being completely genuine and kind to me. That surprised me. I'd expected to see some sort of jealous hate in her eyes. We exchanged some small talk. But I was finding it hard to concentrate. Where was Scott? I was dying to see him. I felt guilty that I wasn't able to concentrate on the conversation well, but it was obvious to me that both Aiden and Alice were only really interested in talking to each other. It was becoming increasingly obvious to me that Alice was in love with Aiden as well. I wasn't sure how he was so blind as to think there might be any doubt in her mind, but I knew it wasn't my place to push him into thinking that.

"Oh, here come Liv and Scott," Aiden said, and I felt my body growing hot. This was the moment. "Hey, guys," Aiden said, and he grinned at his siblings. "Guys, I want you to meet my friend, Elizabeth. Elizabeth this is my sister Liv and my brother Scott."

I know I must have said something, but I can't for the life of me remember what. All I can remember is looking into Scott's narrowed blue eyes as he stared at me. My heart thudded as I took in his appearance. He looked sexy in his black soccer pants and white t-shirt. Too sexy. It was almost too much for me to take. I wanted to reach over and kiss him. I wanted to touch his face. Kiss his lips. Feel his warm, hard body against mine. But instead I just stood still and smiled like a fool. I played football and smiled with Aiden and ignored Scott as best as I could, but all I could think about was the fact that I wanted to go and talk to him. Badly. I was going to make an excuse to go over and talk to him at the end of the game, but as I was about to run over to him, I saw him walking over to Alice and watched them leaving the field together. My stomach lurched as I watched them leaving together, and all I could think about was whether he liked her now. I remembered that they had shared a kiss once. I wondered if he was going to go for Alice, even though he knew his brother was in love with her. I wanted to scream and shout and run after him. I wanted to stop them from leaving together. I wanted to beg him to talk to me, but instead I just walked over to Aiden and chatted with him for a few minutes about what his next plan was and then I left. There was a match the next week, and I was determined to get an opportunity to talk to Scott before this assignment with Aiden was over.

✦ ✦ ✦

"Elizabeth, you know that I love you, right?" Lacey said as we sat in front of the TV that night.

"Yeah, why?" I looked at her suspiciously.

"You need to call Scott."

"What? No way."

"Yes way. There is no way you're going to last until next week, and what if he doesn't talk to you then? What if he leaves early with Alice again?"

"I'll worry about that next week." I made a face at her.

"Call him." She grabbed the remote and paused the screen. "Now."

"You're bossy."

"Here's your phone." She handed me my phone. "I'm not giving you the remote back until you call him. I don't care if that's tonight or in two weeks. No call, no remote."

"You can't last without TV for that long." I made a face at her.

"You wanna bet?" She cocked her head and smiled.

"Fine." I groaned. "I'll call him." I jumped up off of the couch and walked out of the living room.

"And I'm not going to give you the joy of hearing the conversation either."

"Aw, what a pity for me." Lacey grinned. "What ever will I do?"

"Whatever." I shook my head and walked to my bedroom. I closed the door behind me and jumped onto my bed. I lay back and stared at the phone, my heart racing. I wanted to call Scott, but I didn't know what to say. Would he even answer his phone? Would he even want to talk to me? I didn't even know what to do. I closed my eyes and took a deep breath and started punching the numbers in to unlock my phone when I suddenly got a text message. My heart jumped as I saw that it was Scott.

Hey. It was one word, but it felt like an ocean of words.

Hey. I texted him back right away. I wasn't going to play games and wait.

How you doing? he replied.

Okay. You?

Not bad. So you're seeing my brother now?

No. You know I'm not.

Yeah.

I waited to see if he was going to text anything else. This couldn't be the sole purpose of him contacting me, could it?

My phone buzzed. *I told Aiden about Candy Grams. I didn't think he'd hire you. It was the only company I could think of. He wanted to hire someone to pretend to be his fake girlfriend.*

I was basically the only choice.

Figures.

Hope you're not mad.

He loves Alice, you know.

I know. And she loves him as well.

I know.

They should be together. I typed and my fingers shook. I wanted to add, *Just like us.*

You're looking good.

You too.

You don't look like you've been spanked in a while.

You could change that. I held my breath as I pressed send.

I'm still mad at you.

I know.

You totally played me.

I didn't mean to.

You should have asked me what was going on if you had doubts.

I didn't think.

Obviously.

I had a rough childhood. Two messed up parents. It affected me. I'm sorry.

I thought it was your dad that abandoned you?

Yeah, but mom is off as well.

Oh. Sorry.

Not your fault. And not an excuse. It just makes me a bit of a mess in relationships and dating stuff.

Got it.

You have a great family, though. I love Aiden. He's amazing. And Liv seems really funny as well.

Yeah, they're not bad. I'll keep them.

Liv's fiancé, Xander, seems cool too. Why does she call him Mr. Tongue?

Who told you she calls him that?

I heard her saying something to Alice.

Oh. Smh.

What?

You don't want to know.

I do.

Well, I don't want to talk about it.

Why not?

She's my sister.

So?

Think about it!

About what?

Mr. Tongue!

Oh! I started laughing as I realized what Mr. Tongue must have inferred. *Oops!*

Yeah! Ugh! Do not want to think about my baby sister like that.

You're funny.

You're sexy.

Not really.

Yes really!

I grinned as I stared at his last messages. Scott thought I was sexy. Maybe that meant he really liked me after all.

You there or did I lose you?

I'm here.

Can I call you?

I grabbed my phone and called him instead.

"Hey you," he said as he answered the phone.

"Hey," I said softly.

"I can't believe you're doing those acting gigs." He sounded annoyed. "I mean—"

"Scott!" I sighed. "Are we going to start off the call this way?"

"Would you rather it be phone sex?"

"No."

"I'm still mad at you." He sighed. "It was a shock seeing you the other day."

"It was a shock seeing you as well." I took a deep breath. "Did you lose your job?"

"No, but I did get written up." He sighed. "I'd already complained about Helen, so she was fired, but I was written up for indecent conduct on company property."

"Sorry," I said softly. "I shouldn't have done it."

"I'm glad you did it." He laughed. "It was hot. Damn. I still think about it at night." He sighed. "However, what I don't like is the reason why you did it."

"I didn't just do it to embarrass you," I said softly. "I enjoyed it as well."

"I know you did," he said huskily. "You forget I felt your orgasm."

"Scott," I said, feeling embarrassed.

"What?" he said with an amused tone. "Don't tell me you're embarrassed now."

"I'm not embarrassed," I lied.

"Good," he said. "You shouldn't be embarrassed. You should feel proud. Proud of your sexual rebellion, not of your lack of trust in me."

"I know, and I am." I laughed. "Kind of."

"So, should we start over?" he asked softly. "Do you want us to go on a date?"

"Yes, I'd like that," I said softly, my heart racing, but suddenly a fear filled me. A fear that I knew all too well. A fear that had stopped me from going on dates in the past.

"Did you hear that Xander proposed to Liv?" Scott said casually. "Can you believe it?"

"No, I didn't know." I laughed. "I don't really know them."

"Sorry, I always forget that you haven't been in my life longer. I always feel like I've known you forever."

"I feel the same way," I said and closed my eyes, so I could think of his face as we spoke. "Anyway, why are you shocked that Xander proposed to Liv? Didn't you say he loved her?"

"Yeah, but so soon." His tone dropped slightly. "They barely know each other. I love my sister, you know, but I think they should date for a bit longer. I don't think people need to rush into an engagement."

"Oh." I held in a sigh. "How long do you think a couple should be dating before they get engaged?"

"Five years," he said seriously, and my heart stopped. Five years? "You?" he asked me softly, and I wondered how we had gotten to such a serious conversation already. We'd only just got to talking again.

"I don't know, maybe six months to a year." I said.

"Six months?" His voice was incredulous. "What?"

"I think when someone knows, they know. True love and soul mates should be together as much as possible. I see nothing wrong with getting engaged and married quickly."

"Oh," Scott said, and I wondered what he was thinking. Was he regretting calling me now? Was he seeing that perhaps we weren't very compatible? I felt sad at the thought but wanted to be realistic. Maybe all we'd had really was sexual compatibility. Maybe what had happened with Helen had been good for us. Maybe it had saved us both from even more heartache.

"Eliza." Lacey knocked on my door, and I groaned.

"Hold on, Scott, my friend Lacey is at my door."

"Lacey, your best friend that lives with her parents?"

"Yes, but she lives with me now, and she's at my door."

"When did this happen?"

"A few weeks ago."

"A lot changes in a few weeks," he said softly, and I nodded.

"Yeah. Hold on okay?"

"Okay," he said, and I jumped off of the bed and hurried to my door.

"What is it?" I asked her quickly. "I'm on the phone like you told me to be."

"You've got flowers," she said and held a bouquet in front of her. "They just arrived."

"From Scott?" My heart thudded. Maybe this was going to work out after all.

"No," she said softly. "Not Scott."

"What?" I could feel my face going white as I stared at her. "Please tell me these red roses aren't from Aiden." My heart dropped as I gazed at her. If they were from Aiden I'd scream.

"Not from Aiden," she said and pursed her lips. "Check the card."

"Who else would be sending me flowers?" I frowned and grabbed the card. I opened it and read, "A rose by any other name would smell as sweet." I made a face. "Someone likes quoting Shakespeare."

"Read the rest," Lacey urged me.

"But an Elizabeth that wasn't Elizabeth Jeffries just can't hold my heart." I rolled my eyes, but continued reading the card. "I miss you, Shane." My jaw dropped as I realized who'd sent me the card. "Bloody hell! Shane?" I looked at Lacey with a shocked expression. What was Shane doing sending me flowers? He'd been out of my life for two years now. I'd finally gotten over his cheating and my heartache.

"What are you thinking right now?" she asked softly, her eyes studying my face.

"I want to know why he's contacting me. The bloody bastard." I stared at the card and the roses. "Why now?"

"I bet he regrets what happened." Lacey said. "I bet he wants you back."

"There's no way," I said. "Just no way," I said confidently, but something in my heart didn't feel so confident, not now that I was beginning to doubt my compatibility with Scott. "I gotta go back to my call."

"Okay," she said. "I'll be in the living room if you want to talk."

"Okay," I nodded. "I'll be out in a bit." I turned around and walked back to the bed and picked up the phone. "Hey, sorry about that," I said, trying to be cheerful.

"That's okay. What happened?" he said lightly.

"I just got flowers," I said, I wasn't sure why I was telling him.

"Oh?" His voice changed.

"Yeah, from my ex-boyfriend, Shane."

"The one that cheated on you and broke your heart?"

"Yeah," I mumbled. "That one."

"I thought you guys didn't talk anymore."

"We don't," I said, as my mind raced. Why had Shane sent me those flowers?

"So, he just decided to send them tonight? Out of the blue?" Scott's voice was tense.

"Yes," I said. I didn't know what to say, and I didn't know how to explain that Shane and I went back years. That we'd always had a bumpy relationship, but that I'd thought he'd always be there for me. I didn't know how to tell him that as much as I hated Shane, I was still curious about what might have been. I didn't tell him that Shane and I had a history of going back and forth. That I knew what I got with him. That I was scared to venture into new relationships because I was scared of getting hurt.

"You're a woman of mystery, Elizabeth," he said simply.

"Not really. I'm pretty much an open book."

"Do you still love him?" he asked me softly.

"Who?" I said, playing for time.

"You know who."

"I don't know," I said honestly, and the phone went silent. How did I tell him that Shane was the first man I'd ever given my heart to? That I'd thought we'd be together forever? How did I tell him about the nights we'd spent talking about our dreams of moving to Los Angeles and becoming movie stars? How did I tell him that Shane had made me feel like I was capable of being loved and beautiful at a time when I'd felt neither? And how did I tell Scott that when Shane had cheated on me, he'd crushed my heart and soul and made me lose any confidence that I'd felt? How did I tell him that a part of me still longed for the early, easy days of my relationship with Shane because they'd been so perfect? Shane had made me feel so safe and secure in those early days. How did I tell Scott that I was scared of him and giving my heart out to someone new? How did I tell him all of that without ruining whatever new beginning we were forging right now? How did I tell him without him thinking I was too needy and had too many issues? I knew I had emotional issues. I knew I was high-maintenance in a way that most girls weren't. I just didn't think that this was the time to tell him. Not after everything that had already happened with us.

"I see." His voice was abrupt. "So I guess my text and call tonight was pointless?"

"No, I was going to call you as well." I pursed my lips. "I've missed you, Scott."

"Me, or the sex?" he said bluntly. "Or someone to talk to while you've been pining away for Shane?"

"I've missed you, Scott," I said, hurt at his tone and question. "I haven't been pining away for Shane."

"But you don't know if you still love him?"

"I don't still love him." I sighed. "It's not like that."

"Then what's it like?" Scott was annoyed.

"What's your problem?" I sighed. "We're not together. You haven't even spoken to me in a month."

"Because you lied to me and played me, and here I am reaching out to you again, asking you to date me, and you're telling me you're interested in dating another guy."

"I never said that. You're putting words into my mouth." I didn't understand what was happening. What had gone wrong so quickly?

"I gotta go, Elizabeth," Scott said quickly. "Give me a call when you figure everything out."

"Wait, what?" I said quickly, but he'd already hung up on me. I dropped my phone on the bed and walked into the living room and stared at Lacey. She looked up at me with wide eyes.

"What's going on?" She paused the TV and frowned. "You look weird."

"I don't know," I said and stood there with a mind as blank as a blackboard on the first day of school. "I really don't know what's going on, Lacey. I think I'm in the Twilight Zone."

Chapter Fifteen

"You look confused, Eliza." Lacey said. "Shane got you confused?"

"No, but Scott does." I sighed.

"Just Scott?"

"I don't know." I walked over to the couch and sat next to her. "Why me? Why did Shane have to send those flowers tonight?"

"You know how he is. Whenever he thinks he's truly lost you, he tries to reel you back in again."

"It was just the worst possible timing." I sighed. "Scott and I had been talking about how long people should be dating before they get engaged and, well, we really disagreed about the amount of time, and I think that made me a little upset, so I acted a bit stupid when Shane sent the roses."

"What does that mean?" Lacey sat there, her eyes confused. "How did you act stupid?"

"I may have led Scott to believe that I still had a thing for Shane."

"Eliza!" she growled. "How could you?"

"I was confused," I moaned. "I was remembering how it was with Shane when we first started dating. How we used to share our dreams and lie on the beach and make love."

"Eliza." She shuddered.

"What?" I shook my head and let out a huge sigh. "In the beginning it was great with Shane, you know that. I thought we were going to get married. That's something both of us talked about."

"Yeah, because you were both in college." Lacey sounded annoyed. "And he was just saying whatever he could to get into your pants."

"I don't believe that. I think in the beginning he really loved me. He wanted what I wanted."

"Elizabeth!" Her voice rose. "Shane was a jackass. A player. He cheated on you. He doesn't deserve any more second chances. And you know what, you're a jackass too if you seriously think that there is any comparison between Scott and Shane."

"You don't even know Scott," I huffed.

"I know that he's trying. I know that he made you happy. I know that he was fun. He was smart. He had his shit together. He didn't make you feel ugly and not good enough." Her voice trailed off, and we just stared at each other.

"Why did you show me the flowers from Shane?" I asked her softly. "Why did you interrupt my call?"

"Because I thought that would give you motivation to see where things would go with Scott. I know you, Eliza. I know how you like to take the easy way out, if you think you're going to get hurt."

"Well, I guess you're right." I bit my lower lip. "I don't think Scott wants anything to do with me now." I was starting to feel depressed at the stupid way I had handled the conversation. Why had I let my old sentiments towards Shane cloud my thoughts?

"Well, I guess it's lucky for you that you're still working for Aiden Taylor, then? At least you know you'll see Scott at football."

"Yeah, that's true," I admitted, feeling better.

"Or you can take the bull by the horns and go over to his house and tell him you were acting like a fool on the phone."

"Huh? What?" I looked at her in shock.

"Maybe you need to be more proactive, Eliza. Maybe it's time to put yourself out there."

"I know, it's just a scary thing."

"Life is scary." Lacey shrugged. "That doesn't mean you don't live it. Grab it by the horns and ride it.

Yeah, you'll get tossed around a bit and even hurt some more, but ultimately you'll get over it. You know that now."

"That's true." I nodded. "I don't feel hurt when I think about Shane anymore."

"And honestly, Eliza, do you really want to deal with him again?"

"No," I said without hesitation.

"Because?"

"Because I like Scott." I sighed. "And I want to see where it could go with him, even if I fall in love with him and he never wants to marry me."

"So what are you waiting for?"

"You really think I should go and see him tonight?"

"Yes. I really think so."

"Okay," I said and paused. "But if I go, you have to do something too."

"What's that?"

"You have to come to the football game with me next week. There are some cute guys there. You have to attempt to talk to some of them."

"Some of them?" Lacey raised an eyebrow at me. "Not just one?"

"Nope." I grinned, my stomach jumping as my body was already thinking about going to see Scott. "Not just one."

"Fine," she said. "I'll go."

"Good." I jumped up and ran out of the living room. "I'm going to shower and then I'm going over to Scott's."

"Good." She laughed. "I don't expect to see you back here until tomorrow."

"Oh, wait." I stopped and turned back to look at her. "I'm meant to spend the night texting Aiden."

"What?" She looked confused and then her face changed. "Oh God, Elizabeth, you're not falling for Aiden are you?"

"No, no," I laughed, "as part of my job, I'm meant to send some flirtatious texts and ask him to come over for dinner, I'm thinking lasagna or steak, but maybe not lasagna as I texted about lasagna last week."

"Huh?"

"He's going to leave his phone in a room with Alice." I laughed. "He thinks curiosity might get the better of her. In fact, he thinks she might have checked his phone already last week."

"Hmm. That seems like an extreme lie?"

"Well, I guess Alice isn't much better. Back when Scott's sister Liv was dating Xander, Alice hired two strippers and had them go over to Scott's parent's house and pretend they were their dates."

"What?" Lacey burst out laughing. "Are you joking?"

"No," I giggled as I shook my head. "Crazy, right? But I guess I understand why Aiden wants to make sure that Alice is ready for a serious relationship."

"Wow, he must really love her." Lacey's eyes were bright. "He's thought through every single detail."

"Yeah, I guess that he's getting some help from Xander as well." I laughed. "And Liv doesn't even know."

"Uh oh, keeping secrets from his fiancée?"

"I know. I just hope it doesn't blow up on the both of them."

"Yeah, me too." I sighed. "Maybe I'll send him a few texts and then go over."

"Or why don't you just call Scott back and then go and see him later."

"Good thinking." I said. "I'll call him and then text Aiden at the same time."

"What a life you're leading, Elizabeth Jeffries."

"Tell me about it," I groaned. "Not exactly the life I was thinking I'd be leading right now."

"You going to call the number on the card?"

"Shane's card?" I asked her softly.

"Yeah." She looked at me thoughtfully. "I know you're over him, but I also know the hold he had on you."

"Sometimes I just remember those days and I think, why didn't it work?" I leaned back against the wall. "He was my everything, you know. And even though he hurt me, that's not what I remember when I think of him. I think of all the times he drove me to my father's town so I could go and knock on his door. And all the times he drove me home without judgment when I hadn't been brave enough to knock and confront him."

"He was there for you," Lacey acknowledged.

"I cried on his shoulder so many times, and he just held me." I felt myself becoming emotional as I stood there with her. "I just don't understand why he had to cheat on me. I thought he'd always be there for me. I thought we were going to be together forever."

"You loved him." She got up and walked over to me. "And he loved you, but he hurt you, Eliza. More than once."

"I know." I sighed and looked up into her face. "I promised myself that I'd never go back. That I wouldn't let him break my heart again. That he wouldn't make me cry again."

"Then don't."

"I don't want to." I smiled weakly. "I want to get to know Scott better. I want to be strong and just ignore Shane. I know that he's bad news. And I know that I really like Scott, he brings something out in me that I've never had. It's like an evolution of a me that I didn't even know existed. I don't know exactly why I feel this way. I barely know him. But it's about more than sex. There's something about him that makes me just want to be naughty and funny and sexy."

"That's because that's the inner you trying to get out wanting to break free."

"But it's a scary prospect." I played with my fingers. "I mean, Scott has more potential to really hurt me."

"That's because he also has more potential to really make you happy."

"I don't know what to do," I groaned and banged my head back against the wall lightly. "Why do I feel like this? Why am I so wishy-washy? I hate this about myself."

"You can't just change who you are. You have to work on it."

"You mean I won't just wake up one day without all these insecurities?" I joked, and Lacey laughed.

"Unfortunately not. Just like I won't just wake up and find a hot guy in my bed and my book done."

"Well, we can work on both of those." I stepped forward and hugged her. "I'm going to make sure that we get you a good guy, Lacey. You deserve one for putting up with me."

"I sure do." She giggled. "Now, go make your calls and let me write. This hero isn't going to go car racing without me getting him to the track."

"Car racing?" I asked curiously. "Is this still *Play the Player*?"

"Yes," Lacey winked at me. "He's going car racing and then they're going to have sex in the car."

"Sex in the car?" I started laughed. "Oh, Lacey."

"Don't 'oh, Lacey' me. It's going to be hot." She walked back to the couch. "Hot, I say!" she shouted, and I laughed at her as I left the room. I walked back into my bedroom and stared at the red roses on my bed and sighed. I grabbed my phone and called Scott and listened to the phone ringing as I stood there. The call went to voicemail and I hung up. I sat on the bed and waited to see if Scott would call me back, but instead I received a text about five minutes later.

Hey, I don't want to talk anymore tonight. Sweet Dreams.

I stared at the text and sighed. I knew in my heart of hearts that Scott was upset with me. But what could I do? I dropped the phone on the bed and looked at the roses again. It was then that I noticed one white rose and one yellow rose in between all the red roses. I frowned as I picked them up and grabbed my phone to see what a white rose and yellow rose symbolized. I searched and found out that a white rose symbolized new starts and the yellow rose symbolized friendship. And of course the red roses symbolized love. I knew that Shane was sending me a message with his bouquet. A message I should ignore, but as I lay there, I could feel my defenses crumbling. What would it hurt to give him a call? It wasn't as if I were cheating on Scott by talking to Shane. Scott and I didn't have anything. And maybe that was my fault, but I was hurt that he was shutting me out. I lay back and closed my eyes, waiting for a sign from a God as to whether I should call Shane or not. As I lay there an image of Scott popped into my mind, and I started smiling. It was an image of when I was on the desk and he was between my legs in his office. It had been hot and sexy and I was feeling wet just remembering that day. I opened my eyes and looked at the roses and started laughing. Shane didn't match up to Scott, not even a little bit. Yes, Shane and I had a past. Yes, sometimes I regretted the fact that we hadn't ended up together. I missed the fact that he got me and understood me and where I was coming from, but I also knew I couldn't get stuck in the past. That was my biggest problem. I knew that. I knew that, and I didn't want it to control me anymore.

Chapter Sixteen

"This football game is going to kill me." Lacey sounded like she was grunting as she ran up to me. "I can barely breathe."

"It won't kill you." I laughed and then lowered my voice. "See any guys you like?"

"I'm not even paying attention to any of the guys," she said and bent over for a few seconds. "Though now that I've seen Scott, I can see why he has you all hot and bothered."

"*Had* me hot and bothered." I said with a small sigh. "He hasn't called or texted me since last week when we spoke."

"You did tell him you weren't sure if you still loved your ex boyfriend."

"I didn't mean it like that," I groaned. "I just meant that I might still have feelings. And I only paused because I was feeling upset about what he'd said about becoming engaged."

"But he doesn't know that, Eliza. He can't read your mind."

"I know." I said with a frown.

"Come on, girls." Xander ran past us. "Get on the ball."

"Don't mind him," Liv said, rolling her eyes as she caught up to him. "He's just super competitive."

"Sorry, we're trying," I said and grinned at Liv. I really liked her. She was fun and funny, and I thought that we'd be really good friends if we ever got the opportunity.

"We're all trying as hard as we can," Liv said and stopped next to Lacey and I and grinned. "I'm going to take a break with you guys." She laughed. "I'm out of shape or something, but all this running around is making me so tired."

"I know, me too," Lacey said and they laughed.

"Keep going, Alice!" Liv screamed down the field. I looked ahead and saw Alice running down the field with Scott behind her, Xander's younger brother Henry behind him. I could also see Aiden running fast and my breath caught as I watched them all running behind Alice.

"Wow, she's fast," I said feeling impressed as I watched her.

"She's going faster than I've ever seen in her life." Liv laughed and then screamed again. "You've nearly got it, Alice!" We watched as Alice approached the end, and I wondered if Scott was going to catch her in time.

"Touchdown!" Alice screamed, and I saw her throwing the football down on the ground.

"She did it!" Liv screamed. "She did it!"

"Yeah," I said softly, happy for her but jealous when I saw Scott dropping down on the ground next to Alice. I turned to Lacey to make a face, but she wasn't paying attention to me. Instead she seemed to be gazing at someone across the field. "Lacey?" I said softly as Liv went running off.

"Uh, yeah?" She turned to look at me, her face red.

"What's going on?"

"Nothing?" she mumbled and shrugged. "Why?"

"Who were you looking at?" I asked her and then looked in the direction she'd been looking in. My jaw dropped as I saw Henry approaching us. Was Lacey attracted to Henry?

"Hello, girls, how's it going?" Henry ran up to us and gave us a lazy smile.

"We're women, not girls." Lacey said, and I looked at her in surprise. Since when did Lacey have an attitude about being called a girl?

"Well, hello, women, how's it going?" Henry said, his green eyes dancing as he stared at Lacey.

"Good, you?" she said nonchalantly and looked away from him.

"Good." He nodded and then he looked at me. "So you're Elizabeth?"

"Yeah." I nodded. "I'm here with Aiden."

"You're the girl he's using to make Alice jealous?"

"Yeah, how did you know?"

"Xander's my brother, and Xander's helping him." Henry shook his head. "I can't believe that grown men would be just as immature as the women."

"Why? Because women are immature and men aren't?" Lacey said and looked up at him. I wanted to grab her shoulders and pull her back and tell her to calm down. I wasn't sure why Lacey was acting so antsy, but that sure wasn't the way to get a guy.

"Maybe." He grinned at Lacey and then my jaw dropped as he leaned forward and tapped her cheek with his finger. "But that's for me to know and you to find out." He smiled at her, and I watched as his lips curled up in an almost seductive manner and then he stepped back. "I'll see you two women later," he said, and before either one of us could react, he was running away.

"Oh my God, what was that?" I looked at Lacey, my eyes shocked.

"I have no idea." Lacey gazed at me, her brown eyes stunned as she stared at me, her face a bright red. I watched her touching her cheek in the spot that Henry had touched. "I can't believe he touched me."

"He's cute, huh?" I asked her with a small smile. I'd never seen Lacey like this before.

"Yeah, he's okay," she said causally, but I saw her eyes following him down the field.

"Maybe you can talk to him later," I said lightly.

"Why?" She looked at me, her face still looking stunned.

"No reason." I laughed. "No reason at all."

"Where are you going?" she asked me softly as I started walking.

"Time to work." I grinned and showed her my wrists.

"What are those marks?" She frowned.

"Handcuff marks." I giggled. "I had them on all this morning. Aiden wants me to go over to Alice and flash them in her face a little bit."

"What?" Lacey rolled her eyes. "It seems to me that he's worse than her."

"He is going a bit over the top," I laughed. "But you know how it is in love and war. Anything is game."

"I sure hope it works out for them."

"Me too," I said and then started running. "Wish me luck!" I said as I ran towards Alice, Aiden and Scott. My heart was beating fast as I ran towards them, but not because of Alice and Aiden. I was excited to see Scott. I was going to make sure to be light and smile. I wanted Scott to see that every interaction with me wasn't drama.

"Are you okay, Alice?" I frowned as I ran up to Aiden's love. She was on the ground and her face was twisted in pain.

"Yes, thanks." She nodded with a tight smile.

"Good." I grinned at her. "Excellent touchdown, by the way. Best move of the day! You sure showed the guys what's what."

"I try." She grinned back at me and for a few seconds, we were just two friends enjoying a moment. I was really happy that Aiden had chosen such a beautiful but also a kind and funny girl. It gave me faith that sometimes men did get it right.

"Hey, hey, hey, what about my touchdown?" Scott ran up next to me, and my heart stopped for a second as I looked at his grinning face. "I think that my catch was pretty impressive."

"Impressive to whom?" I teased him and shook my head. I could feel the electricity surging between us.

"Everyone on the field." He laughed and looked around. I felt his hand lightly touch mine, and I gazed up into his eyes, wishing I could pull him down into me.

"Hmm, if you say so." I flipped my hair back and his eyes fell to my breasts.

"I do say so." He moved closer to me and I could feel his chest pressing lightly against me. "Didn't you see me?" His voice sounded husky.

"I saw you, and I saw Alice too." My breath caught. "And Alice definitely had the moves of the day." Scott smiled down at me and licked his lips quickly. I felt his hand touching my hip and my breath caught wondering what he was going to do next.

"Hmm," he said finally. "Maybe I'll concede this once."

"Wow, how grand of you." I laughed and patted the front of my shirt down. I could see Alice staring at us, and I remembered that I hadn't shown her my wrists yet.

"Are you ready, Alice?" Aiden was walking towards us, and I quickly flashed my wrists in her face so that she could see the red indentations. I noticed both Alice and Scott looking at the red marks with curious expressions. I stood back, feeling guilty as I watched Aiden helping her up, and then I looked back at Scott, whose expression held a humorous look.

"Back with those handcuffs again, Elizabeth?" He grinned at me.

"It's not what you think," I said, feeling embarrassed.

"Oh?" he said. "What do I think?"

"It wasn't me and Shane or anything," I said, stammering, and his expression changed.

"I wasn't thinking about Shane. Are you dating him again?"

"No," I said. "I haven't spoken to him since he sent the flowers." I didn't tell him that Shane had called me and gotten my mom to call me as well, on his behalf. I didn't tell him that I'd agreed to call Shane later this week, just to catch up. I didn't think that Scott was the right person to be telling about Shane, period.

"Oh?" He cocked his head to the side and studied my face.

"Yeah."

"Interesting."

"Yup." I felt awkward standing there, not knowing what he was thinking.

"Are we the king and queen of one word responses?" he said with a grin.

"Perhaps," I said and laughed. I watched his boyish face change expressions. He went from a light humorous look to a darker, more lustful face.

"What are you doing tonight?" he said and leaned into me.

"Why?"

"Maybe we can play with those handcuffs again?"

"I haven't seen or heard from you since last week. And now you want us to play with handcuffs?"

"Don't you want to play with handcuffs?" He grabbed my wrists and studied the red marks. "I can tie you up on my bed and do wicked, wicked things to you."

"I don't need you to do wicked things to me." I swallowed hard as he pushed his erection into me. "Scott," I said, my eyes wide.

"What?" He leaned down and blew into my ear.

"Scott," I moaned, "we're still on the field."

"So?" The tip of his tongue darted into my ear and I felt his teeth nibbling on my earlobe.

"What are you doing?" I jumped back, my chest heaving.

"You don't want me?"

"Is this just about sex for you?" I said, feeling confused.

"I'm not here to make new friends, if that's what you're asking." He said with a frown. "We've done this your way, and your way sucked. And you told me only last week that you might still want to fuck your ex, so I'm guessing you're not looking for anything serious."

"You're a jerk," I gasped as I stepped back.

"But I'll still pretty good with a pair of handcuffs." He winked and looked down at my wrists again. "Only I won't leave marks."

"Whatever," I said, my face burning as I turned away from him. He grabbed my arm and pulled me back to him.

"We're not done, Elizabeth," he said softly. "Not even a little bit. The last time we were together, you fucked me with abandon. Trust me when I say that that won't be the last time." He dropped my arm then and then smacked my butt hard. "Run off now. You can go," he said in a dismissive tone, and I ran away from him fuming. He was such a jackass, but I was still turned on. I ran over to Lacey, feeling hot and bothered, and grabbed her arm. "We're leaving and we're getting some drinks. I'm so over Scott Taylor."

"I didn't know you were under him," Lacey said and started giggling, but she stopped as soon as she saw the look on my face. I was fuming mad. I couldn't believe how rude Scott had been, especially because he had been so nice and happy when he'd first come over to me. I just didn't understand him. He was almost as hot and cold as I was.

Chapter Seventeen

"I feel so sad, Lacey," I said as I got dressed. "I know I shouldn't. I should be happy for Alice and Aiden. I mean they deserve to be together and to be happy, but I'm sad I won't be a part of their lives anymore."

"Yeah," Lacey looked pretty disappointed herself. "Maybe they'll still be friends with you."

"Even though Alice knows I was an actress paid by her boyfriend?" I said and made a face. "I doubt it."

"You never know." Lacey sat on my bed as I got dressed. "Frankly, I'm surprised that it all worked out for Aiden and Alice. I was pretty sure that she would flip out on him and leave him."

"She's not me." I laughed as I put on a gold necklace. "I guess maybe I'm the only one that goes that crazy over lies."

"Yeah, you're over the top." She laughed. "Well, with the wrong guys."

"Lacey." I gave her a warning look.

"What?" She narrowed her eyes at me. "I don't think it's a good idea that you're going to be speaking to Shane tomorrow."

"You think I should just tell him no?"

"Yes, I do." She nodded. "How are you going to try and see where things go with Scott if Shane is still in your life?"

"It's just a call."

"It's never just a call. You have history with him, Eliza."

"Fine." I grabbed my phone and shook my head at her. "You're ridiculous."

"Have you texted him yet?" she asked with a raised eyebrow.

"Hold on," I sighed and then sent Shane a text. *Hey, it's Eliza. I can't talk tomorrow after all sorry.*

Shane text back immediately. *Tonight then?*

No. Sorry.

Day after tomorrow.

Never, Shane. Sorry.

I have something for you.

What?

Something important. Something special.

I don't want it.

Please Eliza!

I'm sorry. No.

Okay.

I read the texts aloud to Lacey and she groaned and jumped off of the bed. "What's his problem? Why can't he just leave you alone?"

"I don't know." I pursed my lips. "What do you think I should do?"

"I think just ignore him from here on out." She grabbed the phone and looked at it. "What does he have for you?"

"I don't know, Lacey. You know as much as I do."

"I bet it's a bloody ring." She looked pissed. "He's that sort of jerk that would try and propose to get you back now he knows you don't want him."

"It's not a ring," I said, but I wasn't sure. It could have been a ring for all I knew. I sighed as I looked at her. "Why is he back in my life?"

"Because he realizes he fucked up big time, and now he wants you back." Lacey rolled her eyes. "If a guy ever does that to me, I will tell him where to get off."

"Any guy in particular?" I teased her.

"Nope," she said quickly, but her face went red.

"No Henrys in your future?"

"Eliza, stop!" she groaned. "He's an arrogant asshole."

"And you want to do him."

"No, I don't," she said, but she laughed. "Try and take a photo of him and send it to me if you see him tonight."

"No, I won't be doing that." I laughed. "I'm surprised that Aiden and Alice even invited me tonight. It's a family board game night. And they all know that I was never really seeing Aiden. It's so weird."

"And they still don't know that you dated Scott, right?"

"We didn't really date, but no, they don't know we've had sex." I groaned. "Tell me again, why I'm going tonight?"

"So you can see Scott." She laughed. "And find out more information on Henry."

"So you admit, you like him?" I said in glee.

"I didn't say I liked him. I just want some info." She grinned. "Like, is he single?"

"Are you sure you don't want to come tonight?" I asked. "I'm sure Aiden wouldn't care."

"There is no way in hell I'm gatecrashing tonight." She laughed. "Let's make sure everything goes well first."

"Thanks, Lacey," I sighed and looked at my watch. "How do I look?" I twirled around in my new black jeans and white top, and Lacey grinned.

"Very pretty. Have fun and text me when you can. I want to know what's going on."

"Yes, Lacey." I laughed. "I'll see what I can do. See you later." I said and then hurried out of the room and out of the apartment. I was driving to Scott's parents' house. It felt weird to be going to an event with his family without really knowing what was going on between the two of us. My phone started ringing as I got to my car, and I groaned when I saw it was Bob on the phone.

"What do you want, Bob?" I said abruptly. I still had to talk to him about my pay, but I wasn't in the mood to deal with his bullshit.

"I have a job for you," he said, sounding excited.

"Okay?"

"You'll be a dancer for this new club, Go-Go Girls."

"A dancer?" I got into my car and frowned. "For a club?"

"It's a strip club, but you don't care right?"

"What?" I was starting to get angry.

"You'll get $500 a week." He sounded excited. "You only have to work Friday and Saturday nights."

"What does this have to do with Candy Grams?" I said my voice rising.

"Well, I'm the lead on the job." He sounded annoyed that I was questioning him. I listened to him going on about what a good opportunity this was for me and finally just lost it.

"Stuff that job and stuff you, Bob!" I shouted in the phone. "I'm done with you and your shitty jobs and your thieving ways. I quit."

"Wait, what, Elizabeth?" He sounded panicked.

"Seeya, Bob. Lose my number," I said and hung up. I started laughing as I started the car. I was a little worried that I wouldn't have enough money to pay the bills, but I'd find another job. I was so happy to finally be done with Bob. I wasn't even sure how I'd lasted that long with him in the first place.

✦ ✦ ✦

I sat at the dining room table with the rest of the Taylor family, and I couldn't believe how welcoming everyone had been. Especially Alice. Alice was surprisingly friendly and giddy around me, but I supposed that now that she and Aiden were officially together, she had no worries with me at all. I laughed at some joke Xander was making with Liv and I made sure to keep an eye on Henry so I could report back to Lacey all that I found out.

"What do you want to play, Elizabeth?" Liv asked me as she and Aiden argued over Monopoly.

"Who me?" I asked, feeling like I was on the spot all of a sudden. I could see everyone staring at me, and I just sat there not knowing what to say. I looked over at Scott, and he gave me a small smile. "I don't mind. I'm just happy to be here. I'm surprised I was invited." I looked at Alice then. "I wasn't sure how you'd feel about me being here."

"Oh, I'm fine," she said and then laughed. "You were a great actress and I was jealous of you, but you were always nice. I'm glad you're here. Liv and I need another girl in this group."

"Aww, thanks. I'm so happy to be here." I smiled at her and Liv. "I'm so glad to make some new friends in town. My friend Lacey just moved here, but we don't really know anyone else."

"Oh, I thought you made friends quite easily," Scott interjected with a weird look on his face.

"I'm glad I gave you that impression," I said and gave him a look. Was he going to ruin this moment?

"I think we all got that impression, didn't we?" Scott looked around the table, his tone surly.

"I'd be happy to show you around town," Henry said. "And your friend Lacey, if you want."

"I'll ask her, thanks. I'd like that." I grinned at him. Score one for Lacey!

"I'm sure you would," Scott said and then chugged his beer down. "But would Shane?" I heard him say lightly under his breath. I glared at him, but he ignored me.

"You guys want to play truth or dare?" Liv said, and we all chorused "yes." I was glad that she had changed the subject so that Scott didn't continue with his digs. I wasn't sure how it happened, but my question was in relation to my job, and I ended up telling everyone that I was no longer working for Bob and was jobless. I was starting to feel embarrassed for admitting that when Scott spoke up.

"Maybe I can help you with a job." Scott said with a serious expression. "I'm looking for an assistant."

"Oh, really?" I said, my voice light. Oh God, please don't let him bring up my last position as his assistant.

"Yeah." He grinned. "I'm looking for someone trustworthy. Someone I can count on to do her work and not cause trouble in the office."

"Sounds like I could be your girl." I offered him a weak smile.

"Great, we can talk later." He grinned at me as he continued chugging his beer.

"Okay," I said and looked away. My heart was thudding and I didn't know what was going on. Was Scott being serious? We continued playing a few more rounds when suddenly I felt a hand on my shoulder.

"Hey, Elizabeth," Scott said and put his beer down on the table. "I need to get another beer. Want to go and talk in the kitchen while I get one?"

"Uh, okay. Sure." I smiled awkwardly and got up. I saw Alice and Liv grinning at each other, and I knew that they had a feeling that something was going on. "What are you doing?" I hissed at Scott as we walked into the kitchen.

"What do you mean?" he said innocently as he opened the fridge. "Want a beer?"

"No." I shook my head and sighed. "I don't understand you, Scott. What do you want from me?"

"You'll see." He grinned, and I felt his hand on my back, running down to my ass. I jumped and looked out to the dining room.

"Scott, what are you doing?" I glared at him.

"Not much right now." He laughed. "But, do you want to know what I'm going to do to you?" His voice was soft as he leaned towards me and whispered into my ear. My legs shook and my skin tingled at the feel of his warm breath. He didn't wait for me to answer before he continued talking slowly in a seductive voice. "The next time I get you in my bed, I'm going to tie you up so you can't move, then I'm going to spray whipped cream on your breasts and then I'm going to—"

"Scott!" I cut him off, my face going red as Alice and Liv looked over at us from the table with confused and interested expressions from across the room, where they were looking at a photo album from their high school days while they waited on the game to resume.

"Yes, Elizabeth?" He stepped back and smiled at me innocently.

"Stop it," I hissed at him and then smacked his chest when I saw Liv and Alice looking away.

"Stop what?" he said with a smirk and ran his finger across my lips gently.

"You can't do that." My eyes flashed at him as I looked at the two girls again. What was he playing at? Was he going to expose me and the fact that we'd already met? Heat spread across my face and warmed my belly as I stood there in front of him. Oh God, he wasn't going to tell them about our shared past, was he? Not that I cared, but I didn't want them to think I was a bigger liar than I was. Oh, the irony of the situation.

"I think you'll find I can do what I want," he said casually and then leaned back down to whisper in my ear again. "And I think after I've sprayed the whipped cream on your breasts and down your stomach, you'll be begging me to do what I'm thinking about doing next."

"What's that?" I swallowed hard, not believing I was allowing myself to question him. Like I even cared about what he was going to say. Like I wanted his lips on me. Again. I shook my head slightly, to remind myself that I certainly did not want his lips on me again. No, sir. No thank you. I didn't need to feel the incredibly hard and sensuous Scott Taylor sliding inside of me. Not until we'd had a proper conversation. Not until we finally stopped playing these hot and cold games.

"Are you listening to me, Elizabeth?" He blew in my ear and I jumped back suddenly. "Or should I say, Eliza—" he paused and grinned widely, "—Doolittle?"

"What do you want me to say, Scott?" I said, my tone rising as I was unable to stop myself from giving him the reaction I knew he wanted.

"I want you to say that when I fuck you the next time, you won't be playing any games."

"The next time?" My jaw dropped, both at the crudeness of his words and the fact that he thought we were going to get together again.

"Yeah." He smiled and his blue eyes gazed into mine with an amused expression. "Only this time, you'll be the one getting the shock of your life."

"You're not still mad about the lap dance?"

"No." His fingers grabbed mine and he pulled me towards him. "So when can I see you again?"

"Tonight." I said softly, not even sure where the word had come from. I couldn't believe that I was saying it. "You can come over tonight."

"I can?" His eyes sparkled into mine. "You're sure about this?"

"I'm sure that I want you to lick whipped cream off of my breasts, yes." I winked at him. "I mean, we need to talk. I'm not just going to jump into bed with you again. We need to see what we both want and figure this all out."

"You lost me after licking whipped cream off of your breasts," he muttered.

"Scott!" I rolled my eyes at him, but I was already feeling excited. I wasn't sure what Lacey was going to say when Scott and I arrived home together, but I was pretty sure she'd be happy for me.

"What can I say?" He leaned close and gave me a quick kiss. "I've been thinking about touching you and fucking you since you arrived tonight."

"So romantic," I groaned, but I couldn't stop smiling. "People are going to wonder what's going on."

"Let them wonder." He laughed. "Go and get your stuff. We're leaving."

"What? We're still playing games."

"The only games I want to be playing are me inside of you and how many different ways I can achieve that."

"Scott, you're so bad!"

"Not so bad." He grinned. "You wouldn't be inviting me back if I was so bad."

"Yeah, you're not so bad." I laughed.

"Just give me a chance," he said seriously, his face suddenly changing. "I know I like to joke around and I know that I'm forward, but I do like you, Elizabeth. I like you a lot."

"I like you too," I said. "And I'm willing to give you a chance if you're willing to give me a chance."

"I've always been willing," he said with a smile. "Let's get out of here."

✦ ✦ ✦

"Lacey seems nice." Scott sounded distracted as well as we walked into my bedroom.

"Yeah, she's great." I said and pushed him back against the door. "Kiss me, mister."

"You always surprise me, Elizabeth." He pulled me towards him and pressed his lips against mine. "I never know what to expect when I'm around you."

"I'm a bundle of fun, a roller coaster ride of excitement." I grinned and ran my hands down his chest. His body felt warm, and I smelled him in, happy to be so close to him again.

"You've got that right," he said and grabbed my hand and pulled me towards the bed. He looked down at me and groaned. He pushed me back and I fell onto the mattress. I gazed up at him and his face was dark with desire as he pulled off his shirt.

"Sexy." I grinned as I looked up at him. We both paused as we heard the doorbell going off. "Lacey will get it," I said and pulled him down towards me. "Don't worry about it."

"I'm not." He said as he hand moved up and squeezed my breast. "I have more important things to be doing."

"Oh, Scott," I groaned as he pinched my nipple.

"Shh," he muttered as he pulled my top off and I felt him slipping my breasts out of my bra. He moved his mouth down to my breast and started sucking eagerly on my nipple. I lay back with a big smile on my face and I could feel my toes curling as he switched his mouth to my other breast.

"Elizabeth!" Lacey said and knocked on the door.

"Ignore her," Scott said and I nodded, grabbing his hair and pulling him up for another kiss. I wrapped my legs around his waist and moaned as I felt his hardness against me.

"Elizabeth!" Lacey knocked on my door again. "Elizabeth!" She said loudly.

"I'm busy, Lacey!" I shouted back without moving. "Come back later."

"Elizabeth!" she shouted, more insistently now. "You need to come out, you have a guest."

"I'm not expecting anyone," I moaned as I felt Scott undoing the top of my jeans.

"Elizabeth, Shane is here!" Lacey shouted, and I froze. Scott's eyes narrowed as he looked down at me, and my stomach dropped.

"I don't want to talk to him," I said, but I found myself sitting up.

"Elizabeth, you need to come out. Now." Lacey's voice was anxious. "He brought your present with him. I think you're going to want to see this."

"Don't go," Scott said and grabbed my hand as I jumped up off of the bed and pulled my shirt down.

"I'm just going to send him away," I said, but my heart was thudding. Was Shane, the man I'd loved for years, about to propose to me?

"Elizabeth!" Lacey cried. "Please come out. Shane brought your present and it's not a thing. It's a person. You're going to want to come out now." She banged on the door. "You need to come out now. I think I'm going to faint."

"Oh God." My face went white as I looked at Scott. I knew exactly who Shane had brought with him. There was only one person that Shane would bring to win me over.

"Elizabeth?" Scott looked at me with worried eyes. "Are you okay?"

"Yes," I said and nodded slowly. How was I going to tell him the truth? How was I going to tell

Scott everything about me and my past? There was no way he'd understand this. There was no way he'd understand what I'd hidden from him. I didn't know what to say or do. He knew that Shane had hurt me, but he didn't know everything. He didn't know what I'd done. What Shane had done. What we'd done together. I wasn't sure how Scott was going to react when we walked out that door. How he'd feel about me. All I knew was that Shane wasn't going to be going away. And that he wanted me badly. He wanted us to have our happily ever after as well. The only problem was that I didn't know what that was anymore.

FALLING for my BOSS

The End of *Falling For My Boss*.

There will be a sequel called *Seducing My Assistant* that will be told from Scott Taylor's perspective. It is available for preorder now! There will also be a book for Lacey and Henry called *Falling for the Billionaire*, and it is also available for preorder. If you would like to read Alice and Aiden's story, you can read my book, *Falling For My Best Friend's Brother*, and you can read Liv and Xander's story in *One Night Stand*.

Join My Mailing List to be notified when I have new books: http://jscooperauthor.com/mail-list/.

Author's Note

Thank you for reading *Falling for my Boss*.

Please join my MAILING LIST to be notified as soon as new books are released and to receive teasers (http://jscooperauthor.com/mail-list/). I also love to interact with readers on my Facebook page, so please join me here: https://www.facebook.com/J.S.Cooperauthor. You can find links and information about all my books here: http://jscooperauthor.com/books/!

As always, I love to here from new and old fans, please feel free to email me at any time at jscooperauthor@gmail.com.

About the Author

J. S. Cooper was born in London, England and moved to Florida her last year of high school. After completing law school at the University of Iowa (from the sunshine to cold) she moved to Los Angeles to work for a Literacy non profit as an Americorp Vista. She then moved to New York to study the History of Education at Columbia University and took a job at a workers rights non profit upon graduation.

She enjoys long walks on the beach (or short), hot musicians, dogs, reading (duh) and lots of drama filled TV Shows.

Printed in Great Britain
by Amazon.co.uk, Ltd.,
Marston Gate.